SHE

ALSO BY MICHELLE LATIOLAIS

Widow
A Proper Knowledge
Even Now

S H E

fiction

Michelle Latiolais

W. W. Norton & Company

Independent Publishers Since 1923

New York • London

For information about permission to reproduce selections from this book, write to Permissions, W. W. Norton & Company, Inc., 500 Fifth Avenue, New York, NY 10110

For information about special discounts for bulk purchases, please contact W. W. Norton Special Sales at specialsales@wwnorton.com or 800-233-4830

Manufacturing by RR Donnelley, Harrisonburg, VA
Book design by Mary Austin Speaker
Production manager: Anna Oler

Library of Congress Cataloging-in-Publication Data

Names: Latiolais, Michelle, author.
Title: She : fiction / Michelle Latiolais.
Description: First edition. | New York : W. W. Norton & Company, [2016]
Identifiers: LCCN 2016000563 | ISBN 9780393285055 (hardcover)
Subjects: LCSH: Teenage girls—California—Los Angeles—Fiction.
| Runaway teenagers—California—Los Angeles—Fiction. | Interpersonal relations—Fiction.
Classification: LCC PS3562.A7585 S54 2016 | DDC 813/.54—dc23 LC record available at http://lccn.loc.gov/2016000563

W. W. Norton & Company, Inc.
500 Fifth Avenue, New York, N.Y. 10110
www.wwnorton.com

W. W. Norton & Company Ltd.
Castle House, 75/76 Wells Street, London W1T 3QT

1 2 3 4 5 6 7 8 9 0

For Lynette

My extraordinary sister

S H E

SHE

She'd been home-schooled for ten years, and whipped for eleven, and tomorrow she would celebrate her fifteenth birthday. That's why she'd come to Los Angeles, to turn fifteen alone and free in a city she'd never been to before. Learning to add had been learning to collect any denomination of coin or bill until she'd had enough to buy this one bus ticket, and yet even then, after all the careful collection, the evasions, even then Sheriff Curty had been waiting at the bus station in Needles to take her home. She heard him making commands into the radio at his shoulder, then questioning the bus driver, his boot hiked up onto the stoop. "She's five-five about, blonde, blue-eyed, fat as a seal."

She crouched on the floor of the bus, in the sixth or seventh row of seats, her bare knees in gum wrappers and grit. She could sight down the metal legs screwed into the flooring, and she could see the dark horizontal length of his thigh and his hand set down upon it wearing the huge police academy ring.

"She's a minor," Sheriff Curty said. "That means she's under—"

"Nope, officer, haven't seen her," the bus driver said. "I know what a minor is."

"How would you mean that?" the sheriff asked.

A bus arriving from Las Vegas was announced over a loudspeaker and then the announcement of the imminent departure of the bus for Los Angeles. The sheriff's radio crackled, and he spoke into it, and then, because she wasn't alone on the bus, people began to talk and shuffle their feet, and a woman in the seat ahead placed both her wrists over the head rest and gestured as though her hands were just palms floating on water, almost no gesture at all, for her to remain down. Why were they all helping her, she wondered?

"Are you through, officer?" the bus driver had asked, but Sheriff Curty's leg didn't slide off the running board for what seemed like minutes. If he leaned down and looked across the filthy bus floor, she'd be discovered, but her heart had not kicked or glitched. She half-expected this to be a trial run, practice, but then the bus had moved and moved for hours, and then stopped, and she imagined the stone being rolled away from the sepulchral door and she was rising from her seat and walking down the aisle of the bus and emerging into the sunlight and into the huge blue Los Angeles sky interrupted up and around and here and there with buildings. She stood on the asphalt, just shy of the bus door. She wasn't frightened, nor was she resolute. There had been addition and subtraction, fractions and the rudimentary algebra that she loved and wanted someday to study again. There had been the Bible, the history of the Holy Land, and home economics, cooking and sewing, and for these she was grateful as they seemed like skills useful to her, skills that people would pay her to practice. She did not expect a welcome anywhere she went, nor did she have a refined destination beyond this threshold. People in the station thought that perhaps she was lost, that she needed help finding some place or some person who was going to meet her, but she was found really, completely where she needed to be, and she smelled the exhaust of the buses and from somewhere sausages cooking and she saw on the sidewalk beyond the station a small dark man anchoring a vast umbrella of balloons. Her heart beat quietly. Perhaps she was resolute, she thought, perhaps she was. She smoothed down her dress and for a moment, a split second, she regretted the smudges along the sides of her white tennis shoes. She had saved them for this special occasion, and they had been pristine when she had set out this morning, walking to the church on Market Street, and then darting up O Street and the quick trot down West Broadway to the bus station, and still her white tennis shoes were untouched, perfect, the white canvas of hope upon her feet.

The trick that she knew that she was going to have to pull off was her age. Scuffed tennis shoes didn't make her look older, nor the small pink backpack. Quite the opposite, she assumed.

She had been brought up in a clean and ordered house, and looking about, she could see that this was not the part of town she needed to be in, and she watched person after person pull the door of a taxi cab open and fold themselves in and lean across the seat, giving the driver directions. She walked toward the line of cabs, holding back just far enough but listening for the directions being given. Could she recognize any place, or recognize some destination that sounded safe, a place where people lived who needed their chores done, their laundry washed and folded, their linen ironed?

"Figueroa and Wilshire" didn't sound right, nor "Staples Center," nor "USC," but then a tall man in jeans and a

—

leather jacket said, "Santa Monica," and she liked the sound of that, a saint's name even if saints were usually Catholic. "How much?" he queried, leaning down into the cab's window. "Jesus, that's a tab," he said, and then he straightened up and looked around. "Hey," he called to her, "are you going my way? We could share the ride? Are you going to Santa Monica?"

It was a woman saint, too, she thought quickly, or at least she assumed it was, and she could ride with this man and the cabdriver would be there and she would probably be safe and she could see a lot of the city since it seemed as though Santa Monica was farther away than the other destinations she had heard requested. They were up on the freeway, zooming along at seventy miles an hour, and she could see blocks and blocks of warehouses and then cityscape, and blocks and blocks of that, and then they passed over another huge freeway with cars jammed up on both sides and then there weren't so many tall buildings and she knew that she had made the right decision.

"Where you going?" he asked, though he had been silent, gazing out his window. She could smell the leather of his jacket, and his hair had been washed that morning and the smell of the shampoo freshened the cab. He had long jeaned legs ending in beautiful worn cowboy boots and something in the old deep creases on those boots she wanted to be able to re-create, distance and time in something she owned, something fine that she had chosen for herself and then worn and worn and worn.

"I have very little money," she said, her voice quiet, precise, half-expecting his hand to come flying. "In fact," she said, "I have almost none at all."

He turned on the seat and looked at her for the first time, seriously, carefully. He had old old eyes, darkened with something they had lived through, but he seemed about forty to her, or maybe fifty. "Somehow I knew that," he said finally. "But it doesn't answer the question of where you're going, does it?"

"Not specifically," she said.

He laughed and turned his head and looked out the window again. When he turned back to her after a time, he had concern in his eyes and cheeks.

"A woman on the bus gave me this card," she said, "but it's not a place." Tentatively she held the small green card out to him, and he took it in his right hand, his eyes casting down quickly, reading. He knew she was telling him something, and she knew that he was deciding whether to hear it or not. He drove his thumb quickly beneath the card and flipped it over and read the other side and then held it back out to her between two fingers. If she had ever seen cards being played, or a high-stakes poker game in Las Vegas, she would have known this particular dexterity meant something. Instead, it seemed brisk to her, dismissive. That's fine, she thought, she could take dismissive, could easily walk away from that, unharmed, free. Los Angeles went on and on all around her.

"So, call the hotline," he said, facing forward, exhaling, and then he said quietly, almost to himself, not looking at her, "but you can't, right? You're practically as far off from eighteen as I am."

—

She held the green card in both her hands, her wrists laid down along her thighs. "I think they're trying to make this sound like First Corinthians. Love is this, love is that—love is trusting, love is caring."

"I think they're more concerned with what love isn't."

"The Bible praises plenty of what love shouldn't be, too," she said. "You could read Leviticus."

"No thank you," he said curtly. He reached back over and took the card from her and read, "Love is not shoving, slapping, choking, hitting, intimidating or threatening you with weapons." He thrust the card back into her hands. "Bible praises that?" he asked, frustrated, but she could see that suddenly he wanted to ask her many questions, that something had switched on in him, or enlivened him. "They'd return you, wouldn't they?" he asked, and he looked at her with his somber eyes. "Child protective services, or some such shit. Harboring a minor. Isn't that what we call it? They insist on having all the fun," he said wryly.

The cab was slowing, changing lanes and moving toward an off-ramp and then they were stopped at a light. The turn indicator ticked and the cabbie fingered something into the keypad mounted on the dashboard.

"I don't know," she said. "If it says 'anonymous and confidential help,' how can they return—?"

"—and what would that be like, being returned? What would be there when you got back?"

She knew that he knew the answers to his own questions, that they were being asked in order to stall, to allow

—

6

him time to think, and to evade this situation, but she didn't really want much from him, other than this cab ride. "I came away from it," she said. "That's what matters." She smiled hugely at him, almost laughing. She wasn't an idiot, she'd find a way to live, to exist. She wouldn't ever be under her father's roof again, and her body, sitting simply on this broad bench seat, was new to her, full of air, fat as a seal, she heard in her mind's ear, fat as a seal! but no matter how fat Sheriff Curty thought she was, he hadn't found her crouched on the dirty floor of the bus—he hadn't dragged her up from between the seats to stand before her father and his deft rapid-fire hand.

"I'd like to see the seals," she said. "There's the ocean, right? There are seals in it, right?"

"Sea lions," he said.

"Those are seals, aren't they? A kind of seal?" she asked.

"Hell," he said, "they can be any damn animal you want them to be. You've come to Lotus Land," and then he laughed, too, his deep amused baritone. She smelled his lovely shampooed hair again and they both gazed out at the blue green expanse of water, mesmerized.

"Just there," she said, pointing. "Would you just let me out there? And maybe, I don't know, maybe in another time, I could pay you back for the ride."

He watched her loop one strap of her pink backpack over her shoulder, the small bulk of it hanging to her hip, and then, looking both ways but not back at the cab, she stepped down into the crosswalk and made her way across the broad boulevard and up into the park along the cliffs that overlooked the ocean. The hem of her dress played at the back of her legs, and then a family of tee-shirted tourists moved alongside her, and when they had passed, there were the rose bushes and a pepper tree and two cyclists leaning against their bicycles, gazing out to the sea. She was gone. "Jesus," he thought. He wasn't fucking watching the local news for the next few days. He didn't want to know when she got added to the body count. He raised his eyes to see the cabbie eyeing him in the rearview mirror, not so much a "can I drive on now?" but a look of uncomfortable resignation much like his own.

The tree that she stood behind watching the cab pull away from the curb and move slowly down the boulevard had long fronds that reached almost all the way to her knees. Small red orbs hung in the fronds and were strewn here and there across the lawn. Within the tree's green cover she watched the green and white cab halt quickly. She expected the cab's back door to swing open and for the man to straighten himself briskly off the car seat and to bound across the street and into the park, but a single small wheel extended from in front of the cab and then she knew the cab had stopped for this cart or stroller, and for the woman pushing it in tight athletic clothes stretched taut across her lean body. She had never worn anything but a dress. She read on the door of the cab both the words "independent" and "united." She thought to herself that she wasn't the sharpest knife in the drawer, but that didn't make all that much sense, and then the cab drove on and for the first time she breathed the sea air in deeply. It begins, she said to herself, and the woman jogged down the broad sidewalk pushing the odd cart that held a baby. She could see that now as the woman moved closer, she could see the baby's small round face jiggling beneath its white cotton hat. She had perhaps made a mistake, she thought. It was cold here overlooking the ocean, and she realized, yes, of course, it would be damp this close to water. She shrugged her shoulder to swing down her backpack. Unzipping it, she drew a pale yellow sweater from its nylon folds and then itemized the pack's scant contents: the black wallet that had been her grandmother's, the jersey nightgown, her two pairs of cotton underwear, a toothbrush and a baggie with toothpaste squeezed into it, a red plastic comb, and one roll of toilet paper that would have to serve all her needs. Enough sanitary napkins would have been too bulky, would have drawn too much attention to her backpack this morning, and she was not allowed Tampax for reasons she both understood and did not. "You're just going to the House," they would have said, either her mother or her father, if her backpack had appeared overly full. "What's in there that you need in the Lord's House?" Her mother might have pulled it from her shoulder and handed it to her father for inspection, but she had carefully packed it so that it looked almost empty, and then had left it on the floor of the living room, just around the corner of the doorjamb, and then she had walked into the kitchen for breakfast, her father already seated, eating, and her mother standing in an apron wrapped around her robe. She wanted to eat a lot, to set herself up for the day, but she was also afraid that this would draw attention, too, and attention of almost any kind provoked suspicion, possibility, and within possibility lurked always something worldly and evil. But she liked to eat and cooking made her mother happy, or so it seemed at any rate, and her mother that morning had offered her a warm plate with small pancakes and a fried egg with its cooked white dotted with black pepper. Her mother said, "Your father's saved you some syrup," and the statement had angered her intensely, nonsensically, she thought to herself, but she said, "Thank you" to her mother and walked around the back of her father eating and pulled the chair out from the table and moved it a bit away from him before sitting down. Her father aligned the chairs at the kitchen table after everyone was up, moving the two along the sides closer to his at the head, close enough for swinging should he feel the impulse. Both her mother and she slid their chairs down as surreptitiously as they could when they sat down; both she and her mother hunched as they ate, and now, standing beneath the tree with its beautiful fronds, she said aloud, "Straighten up. That is over. Straighten up," and she did, breathing in hugely this time and putting her arms slowly into the sleeves of her sweater, feeling every inch of its small warmth as it came upon her. She wanted to remember this, wanted to be so thankful and to remember her own gratitude, to be within bounty so small and precisely adequate that the lesson would sustain her for three years. She knew this, felt this, recognized the moment, though not in words because the words were few, were really just two words, and they were "three years." Three years to make do as well as she could, and then she would no longer be a minor. She could never be returned to them.

She wanted to find a bakery, but first she walked to the low fence that ran along the cliff and looked out over the gray ocean. In the distance, the bobbing black figures seemed to be surfers, not seals, but she felt elated. He had said they could be any animal she wanted them to be, it was Lotus Land, and she smiled at her seals who would occasionally stand up on a board and mount a wave before they were tumbled back into the curly white roil of the water hitting the shoreline. Such smart and agile seals, and she thought that maybe someday she'd own some of this taut clothing, too, and she turned and walked back across the lawn to the sidewalk, her tennis shoes two small white geographies moving beneath her.

Across the boulevard, which she now knew was named Ocean, she looked in the windows of restaurants and through foliage at the semicircle drives of high-rise hotels and then she walked a block of art galleries. She stopped finally and stood gazing at the huge canvases in one long window. She hadn't seen a lot of paintings in her life, but she had never seen a painting signed with the time of day. These all had a name: Giamatti and then 5:15 A.M and Giamatti 4 P.M., and Giamatti 7:13 A.M. She didn't really know why this struck her as so strange, but it did, like a time of death. It seemed so definite, and somehow the opposite of why anyone would paint a picture. But maybe not? Look at the paintings, she instructed herself. Was there a reason in the paintings for noting the time of day? They were all dark spikey skylines with billboards and huge words

—

on buildings in neon, and the paintings looked to her like pages from a comic book she had once seen blowing across her dusty street in Needles. She'd run after the comic book and grabbed it up and turned the lurid pages, taking in their many frames, fascinated by the wide fraught faces of the characters against the lurking urban evil. Her father pulled it from her hands as he walked up behind her.

"It's just a comic book," she had said.

"It's worldly," he replied, and he had rolled it in his hands and then hit it against his palm as he walked beside her. She could hear in her memory the empty smack, smack, smack.

Now, she realized that a woman was just beyond one of the canvases, standing in a tight sleeveless dress and high heels. The woman did not smile, but acknowledged her on the sidewalk, gazing in. The woman had very straight black hair that fell to her shoulders and glanced off them. After a moment, the woman turned and walked to a table, white and angular and bare at the back of the room. Then the woman walked past the table and into a back room and then returned with a tall clear vase of calla lilies, their thick green stems magnified by the glass. The woman kept walking around the table, resituating the vase, leaving it finally in a far right-hand corner. This is when she noticed the hem of the woman's dark dress coming unstitched in back. She could fix that hem in no time. The woman was beautiful and cold and untouchable and she could fix her dress. She swung her pack around and balanced it on her bent knees and drew her grandmother's black wallet from it. In a zippered interior pocket she found the flat card wound with different colors of thread and crossed with a single silver needle. She owned one needle, she thought, even though she came from Needles. She didn't smile or laugh; she just thought it as she zippered up her case and then pushed in through the gallery's heavy glass door.

"Excuse me," she whispered, and then she found her voice. "Excuse me," she said more loudly, and the woman moved toward her. "Your hem is unstitched in back and I could sew it back up very quickly if you'd let me." She held the needle up and the small card of threads. "I couldn't tell from the street if your dress was dark blue or black—black, yes, and it wouldn't take long at all. Maybe a few dollars. I'd appreciate the work—see, there, it's coming out," and she pointed as the woman craned her head back over her shoulder and kicked her leg out behind to raise the hem of her dress so that it draped across her calf.

"Oh," the woman said. "It is pulling out, isn't it. Fuck me."

The language shocked her but she just started unfurling black thread from the card and threading the needle. "Do you have a pair of scissors," she asked. "I could use my teeth, but it'd be neater if I had scissors, a cleaner cut."

The woman stood staring at her with her eyes scrunched up and her lips pushed out in puzzlement. The woman was almost human, and then almost smiling. "Okay," the woman said, her face relaxing. "Let's go in the back. This is really weird."

She followed the woman's stride across the cool room that smelled of recent paint and then they were in a back office and beside a desk and she went quickly to her knees and motioned for the woman to turn around. The woman held a pair of long-bladed scissors in her hands. "I'll just hold these until you need them, in case you try anything funny," the woman said over her shoulder, her eyebrows raised.

"I won't. I don't. I just need work, you know. Work." She could smell the woman's nylons and her perfume and the dress fabric was warm in her hands and she worked quickly, feeding the needle in and drawing it out, pulling the thread taut and smooth, and then again and again, perfect small strokes, and then it was done and she pulled the scissors gently from the woman's hand so as not to alarm her and cut the thread and raised herself off the floor. She turned the scissors so that she handed them back with the blades pointing at her waist. "Is it a little strange," she asked, "that the paintings have a time of day on them? I'm just curious—I just don't know."

The woman looked amused now and tossed her head and said, "I've never thought about it." She bent down and pulled the bottom drawer of a desk open and reached her purse from it. The woman raised the wide front flap of the narrow purse and lifted out an orange wallet. Her straight black hair swung forward and then back. "I never carry much cash," the woman said.

"Just a few dollars," she said to the woman. "It would help a lot." She smiled and she wanted to tell the woman that tomorrow was her birthday, that she would be fifteen, that she would wake up somewhere—she did not know where yet—but somewhere and she would not be sad or afraid or anxious: she would be fifteen and everything would be different and good and it would be the beginning.

—

"We have an opening tonight," the woman said, holding her wallet.

"What is that," she asked her, "an opening?"

"A reception," the woman said. "We've just hung this show, and tonight's the reception. The artist will be here. You could ask him your question." The woman remained looking at her, the wallet in her hand.

"I don't think I like the paintings," she said. "Do you?" Then she realized that perhaps she shouldn't have said that, that in truth she wanted to know more about the paintings. "Could I change what I just said," she asked. "I really don't know enough to like or not like them."

Finally the woman opened her wallet and drew out a five-dollar bill. "Curiouser and curiouser," the woman said, holding the bill out to her.

"I don't have any change," she said.

"But I don't want any change," the woman responded, her wallet snapping shut in the small office. She bent down to place her purse back in the desk drawer. When the woman rose and turned, the heavy glass door of the gallery reflected—as it was swinging closed—cars and people walking. A little plump to be on drugs, the woman thought to herself, but the phone beeped quietly and she reached for the handset.

She had waited for fruit to ripen on the trees in a garden in Needles, figs and loquats and oranges and kumquats. She had never been in this garden, nor exchanged any language with the man who tended it, but she had liked watching this garden

—

15

her entire life. She assumed there would be fruit on the trees in Los Angeles, too, and that a few pieces plucked here and there would not be noticed, or more important, would not be noticed as stealing. She wanted to find a bakery, but perhaps walking until she found homes with gardens was wiser right now. It was cold by the ocean and she hadn't thought about that, and though she now thought to move away from the sea, she also felt invited to the reception tonight, the opening, as the woman had called it, where the artist would be. She could ask her question. "Why the time of day on your paintings? Time of completion? Did paintings get completed so definitively? Like a death?" What time would an opening be, she wondered, and it all seemed odd to her, "opening," when the paintings seemed timed down to the minute. Reported missing at 10:30 A.M. this morning from Needles, California—that was the sort of thing that got a specific time attached to it, not a painting, but even then the specificity of time seemed a false importance. What did it matter if it was 10:30 or 2:30? Just how much weight was there to yet another girl running for her life? There were lots more where she came from, and most of those were staying put. Give those girls a time, a specific time, and they'd be there. Good girls.

She turned up a street and started away from both the broad boulevard named Ocean and from the ocean itself. Trees lined the street densely and she felt their bower, and yet the buildings were apartment buildings and what she imagined might provide her food and perhaps even some back passageway or guest cottage in which she might sleep for the night were homes, residences, estates where she might not be noticed so readily.

—

16

Sure alarms, she agreed, and dogs, sure, but she loved dogs and thought that she might be able to constitute herself so quietly, to appear so unthreatening that barking seemed unnecessary, and she persuaded herself up the long gray narrows of sidewalk. Dogs would like her, would lick her hand and stand beside her and lean against her shins, their coats warm and coarse. They were the best alarms. People preferred them, and these alarms would adore her. She realized that having something to feed a dog would be a smart approach, and she kept a lookout for something edible that had been tossed away. You're not going to find a t-bone steak just lying in the street, she chided herself, but she kept looking nonetheless, for a half-eaten hamburger, even a piece of doughnut or muffin, but the streets were so very clean, pristine, the stuff of her imagination, really, such immaculate promise. Los Angeles.

She wished her tennis shoes clean as she walked, pushing the toe of each shoe forward, as though this action were washing, scrubbing. I don't know, she teased herself, they don't seem much better, those smudges, and then she looked up into the face of a police officer. Where had he come from? and come from so impossibly quietly? but she now saw the police cruiser angled in to the curb and his partner sitting in it, his muscled arm in its short blue-black sleeve gesturing out the window for her to stop. She did. Of course she did. What, she had a choice? She hated pretenses of freedom, pretenses of choice. She walked to the car's open window. The other officer loomed at her side.

"Hi, I'm Officer Luano—this is Officer Kalin. You haven't seen a man with a small white dog, have you?"

—

"He was walking it?" she asked, "or he was stealing it?"

"Nothing lost on you," Officer Luano said. He raised his eyebrows to her and she didn't know if he meant this sarcastically or as a compliment. "He might have been doing one to make it look like he wasn't doing the other."

She thought this might be true of Officer Luano, too, that he was phrasing a compliment to mask his sarcasm?

"I haven't seen anyone," she said. "I mean, I haven't seen anyone with a small white dog. Could I have your card in case I do? I could then call you from my house."

Officer Kalin leaned against the cruiser, his elbows on the white roof. "You live nearby?" he asked, looking out across the street, but it sounded like a statement. Officer Luano was flicking her a card out the window. She took it, saying thank you, and started up the street, their eyes on her back like heated prods. She didn't think policemen got involved with lost dogs, but she wasn't sure, either. She had no identification; she had made sure of that, and no one could make her tell them where she had come from, or her name, or how old she was, but they could arrest her, she supposed, and hold her, and make her live somewhere that she had not chosen. Foster care. She didn't know if that would be terrible or not, didn't know if that wasn't what she should do. She looked back quickly and she could see the officer on the street looking at a Xeroxed picture and then looking up the street and catching her looking at him. She had not considered this simple thing, a photograph sent by fax. Where had a picture of her even been gotten? There were no school pictures, and her parents didn't own cameras, instruments of vanity and pride. It had not occurred to her before that a photograph—wherever they had found one—might be sent out with an "all points bulletin," wasn't that what they called it, of a young girl who had run away . . . a face so remarkably like hundreds of other Caucasian faces, she reasoned, talking herself down. Blonde, blue-eyed. How many of those could there be in California alone? Unless she'd been abducted, or actually, unless her father could make the police believe she'd been abducted, and she didn't think he could because he'd slip up and say Satan at some point, and call her evil. She didn't think the police would even attempt locating yet another girl fleeing her Bible studies for a few days.

She turned and stepped down into the street and crossed and started up a side street so that their eyes could no longer follow her. She walked down the sidewalk in and out of sunlight, trees, no trees, not hurrying in case they managed somehow still to be watching her. At the corner, she glanced at the street names and turned east and started up Idaho and then there was an alley lined with huge lidded bins, and she crossed Idaho at an angle and entered it. Once, a few years ago, she had found a novel beneath a bench at a bus stop and in it the criminals were always entering alleys. You entered an alley, but not a street, she thought to herself, wasn't that interesting. You were just on a street, but entering an alley took willfulness, maybe even ill intentions! She didn't think evasiveness was "ill intentions," but she finally looked at the officer's card, and at the police seal, State of California, with its ocean waves in the background and the small brown bear in the foreground.

—

Officer Alberto Luano. She was collecting cards, she mused, the green card that was the hotline for First Corinthians, "love is not shoving, slapping, choking, hitting," and now this white card with its bear striding before the waves. It was a little bit of a house, these cards, a kind of resort of mind, all the do nots and the dos, a number for faith and a number for the law, a rock and a hard place, but she was in her narrow neat alley, passing through, evading both.

GAS

She stood on the cement island, not far from the black hose and the metal nozzle fueling her car. Her head was tilted up, reading a small mounted poster, her lips rising into a smile. *A Children's Guide to Splattered Bugs*. She laughed and shook her head in amazement and then looked at the numbers undigitizing as quickly as they digitized on the face of the gas pump, and then her head tilted back up to reading the poster. Five-ten or -eleven, he thought, tall! and yet he wondered if she was a dancer. She had a kind of liquid agility in her body that seemed to him in his few brief moments of observation to derive from physical discipline, ballet, he thought, diving—those legs held perfectly long and straight, Barbie doll legs, in a swan dive. He saw this in his head as clearly as if it played out before him on the television, the Summer Olympics, her tall, trained body against the blue of sky and pool. Finally he looked to see what she was reading, the poster. What was so funny? The definitive click and halt of the gas pump sounded, and she swooped down from the island and disengaged the heavy nozzle from her car and lifted it back into the pump. She screwed her gas cap on still looking at the poster, screwed it past two clicks, and then as the strip of white extruded, she ripped her receipt across the serrated edge and walked around and was about to fold her legs into her car when he said, "Do you have a favorite splattered bug?"

—

"I'm sorry," she said, looking seriously at him, her left hand holding the edge of the door. There were rings there, but he couldn't exactly read them, a school ring with a seal, it looked to be, and another, studded with small blue jewels.

"I saw you were interested in the guide to what's smearing up your windshield."

"Oh," she said. "Well, it passes the time while one is—" and then she laughed fully, a bright, hysterical laugh. "The verb to pass is probably a little dicey in a gas station." She sat down in her car and started to pull her door closed. He reached out and held the door and knew the moment he did so was a huge mistake, a step too far, aggressive. Her face was stricken, her eyes instantly dark. He pulled his hand back as quickly as he'd used it to stay her door.

"I'm sorry," he said. "It's just—you'll be gone and I'll never have another chance. Thirteen million people in this burg, you'd be hard to find."

"Find for what?" she said, pulling her door from his hand, though not closing it completely. He saw her right palm laid across the horn, preparing to press it into blaring if need be.

"Just a few minutes. A cup of coffee over there perhaps," he said, pointing at the busy café across the street. "Ten minutes more realistically. Look, there's even parking—I just need someone to talk to."

She hesitated, turned her narrow wrist toward herself, looked at her watch.

"That sounded pathetic, didn't it?" he said.

She lifted her head and gazed through the windshield of

her car. "I was thinking it sounded pathetic and honest at the same time."

"A winning combination?" he ventured, and she laughed again, her high, bright laugh. "I'll meet you over there," he said. "Right?" She didn't answer and he said it again: "Right?" He knew his good jacket and turtleneck and loafers settled her mind a bit, but he also thought her stupid for letting them do so, for operating on such slight assurance. Then again, she still hadn't answered. She pulled her door closed, and he listened to her car starting, the doorlocks clicking down, and watched as she pulled out of the station and onto the street. His gas pump shut off and he stepped up onto the island and across to his own car and placed the nozzle back into the port of the gas pump. He didn't wait for his receipt, his eyes trying to follow her car as it waited in a left-hand turn lane and then made a U-turn and pulled alongside parked cars and then backed slickly into the place in front of the café. She could parallel park a car, and this impressed him even further, somehow this skill, too, part of that physical discipline he perceived striated in her body. He started to get into his car, a used hybrid bought off one of the rental car sales lots, and then he remembered to replace his gas cap. Across the street, her car door hadn't opened yet and he noticed an open-front bar next to the café with men drinking beers and looking out onto the street. He screwed into place his car's gas cap, the black plastic unsatisfying in his hand, almost weightless. He watched the traffic surge by in the solid after-noon light. He could see no other parking near the café. He'd do well to park on this side of San Vicente, he thought, and just

—

walk across. In his car, a Mozart piano concerto ended and then Springsteen sang about an America far from Los Angeles. He loved the shuffle function on a disk player, and when he looked to turn out of the gas station, there was a parking space opening up a half block down, a red Mercedes station wagon angling itself into traffic, and he pulled up behind, his blinkers ticking, and then he parked as deftly as she had. Maybe she was watching. He twisted his rearview mirror ten degrees. He could see that she still had not gotten out of her car.

Perhaps she was hunting for quarters? He pushed back his ashtray cover and ferreted out enough quarters for both their meters. He got out and clicked his car locked, fed his own meter the twenty-four minutes it needed to make up an hour, liked his luck today, slid the other quarters into his jacket pocket, and then waited for three cars to pass down the street so that he could cross. He was just lifting his foot up onto the curb of the grassy median when her car door opened and she stepped out, one long leg beginning to straighten, her blonde hair owning the bright sunlight, and then his view was blocked by a white panel truck and he waited on the median, his polished loafers against the green grass.

The traffic light at the corner had released another surge of cars, and when he managed to get across finally, he realized there was something he should be seeing. A small crowd of people had collected and the driver of the white truck was taking his baseball hat off and holding it against his chest. She was tall against her open car door, the truck hood holding her there, her head thrown back. He was surprised he hadn't heard it, but that was the city, so much noise it was silence really. The patrons from the bar were tumbling out, rushing to help, and he waited for them to clear the entry and then he took a seat on one of their bar stools along the front, his shoes hiked up onto the foot-rail. He had an hour on his meter, and he could see that with her neck like that, she was no longer alive.

"Yeah," he said to the waitress when she appeared, "thanks."

"There are people already sitting here," she said, her hand open, gesturing at the glasses of beer lining the high table. "How about a seat at the back bar?" she offered, but her worried eyes looked out onto the sidewalk.

"Regulars?" he asked. "People who come here always and sit watching the traffic?"

"Right now they're trying to help that poor woman," she said, pointing and then looking back at him curiously. "You're not a doctor, are you?"

"No," he said, "no, I'm not. I think I need one of those myself, along with a Scotch."

He smiled at her, trying to get her attention because her gaze was once again on the woman held up against her car door and the commotion of people on the sidewalk, a number of them on cell phones. The truck driver now sat on the curb, his head in his hands. The traffic merged quietly into one lane and moved slowly around the white panel truck. "You own this bar with your husband?" he asked. The waitress wore a long black dress with a tie in back and the rayon fabric bunched and tucked around her figure.

"And you know that because I'm not some young hot cocktail waitress?" She said this distractedly. "How else could some-one hire me?" she asked, looking pointedly back at him. "You'll have to move to the bar."

"Sure," he said, twisting around, his elbow knocking a glass of beer over, the beer surging into a cataract, splattering against the tiled floor. He slapped down the four quarters from his jacket pocket, stepped around the puddle of beer and out onto the sidewalk.

She looked at his departing back, his glance toward the woman, some minute adjustment in his shoulders, and then his progress across the street, sidling deftly between the slowed cars and then up onto the green grass of the median.

SHE

She walked up and down the groomed residential streets until she'd found a loquat tree, and there it stood, in a small fenced-in yard. Loquats. Clusters of pink-yellow orbs centered within long dark green leaves, and ripe—they appeared ripe. The yard had a lemon tree, too, and a hedge along the side of the driveway that continued all the way to a garage. The garage was its own structure and she wondered if it was locked. After dark, she could perhaps make her way down the drive and into the garage, where she might be able to spend the night under cover. She could see there was a side door into the garage from the back-yard, a small terra-cotta–tiled eave over it. Could she manage to get past the windows of the house undetected? She knew she had the advantage of being just a girl. People's backs weren't up immediately. *Just a girl.* What wrongdoing could a girl get up to? People focused more on what could befall a girl, and she'd heard all about that for years and years, and had decided not too long ago that what could befall her might indeed fall, but that this was also a world of her parents' making, this forest of constant threat, this fable.

She looked at the car parked in the drive, a small white sedan. It was parked in such a way that she felt she knew it was not the car that belonged to a person who lived in this house. The car was parked too shy of the back door, and seemed a bit shabby, but she couldn't trust any of these perceptions exactly, and she knew this. A whirring was coming from a clothes dryer vent near the back door, and she noted that standing by certain vents could get her warm, and she was cold, colder than she realized she'd be. She ambled down the driveway, sidling alongside the car, and then she crossed over the drive and kept close to the walls of the house, gazing in the windows as though she knew who lived there, was looking in! *just wanted to say hello*! What was lost, she thought to herself, if she just knocked on the door and asked if she could pick some loquats? Would she draw so much more attention to herself for doing the right thing, for asking instead of just taking them, instead of just stealing? Her sight took her across a dining room and into a front room where an old man sat in a chair reading a book, but calling to someone, too, someone deeper inside the house, perhaps in the kitchen. Then a man emerged holding a small tray with a bowl of soup on it. He shook his head of black hair and the old man raised both his hands, giving up, it seemed, and put the book down beside him in the chair. He settled the tray on the old man's lap and then she could not see where he went, and they continued to call back and forth at each other but she couldn't exactly make out what they were saying, and then a door opened at the side of the house and she was caught in his dark brown eyes, the steamy heat of the dryer vent warming her. "*Bueno*," he said, a tone in his voice *it's about time you came to visit your grandfather*. "Yes," she said, fumbling, stalling, and then she said, "I'm sorry," because she often said this, in doubt, or just in case, *I'm sorry*.

"No, wait." He held car keys. "You're not Olivia."

—

"Her friend—she's coming, and I'm meeting her here. It's okay, you could go, or no, no, what does he need?" she quickly asked. "Tell me that first. I could do the laundry."

He looked at her now even more closely, bouncing the keys in his broad hand. She understood immediately that offering to do the laundry had given her away. "Just to be useful," she said, "while I wait for Olivia. I could fold." Then she ventured into what she hoped was shared territory: "Olivia's always late."

"Yes," he said soberly. *"Sí."* He held the side door open for her. He smelled good as she passed him, a woody cologne, and then he pulled the door closed and she stood alone on the blue tile of the service porch. She smelled warm suds and heard the low trickle of water filling a washing-machine drum; he had already begun another load, and stacked on the dryer were folded white sheets and pillowcases. His car started and it whined out the driveway as he backed up. She was thinking quickly, wanting to find a house key, and then perhaps a closet where she could hide, stay for the night, she wouldn't hurt anything, would take almost nothing, wanted just a roof over her head, shelter for a night to gather herself into her fifteenth year. A house key, an extra one in a bowl by the door, or in a small drawer near a telephone, or at the back of the old man's top dresser drawer. He would have a dresser drawer, yes, she knew he would, and there would be pictures of his wife and children, perhaps a dish of change, quarters primarily, quarters that she would not take, and maybe a picture of Olivia, or no, she thought, that picture would be framed and on top of the dresser. She thought to find some mail, something with the old

—

man's name on it, a last name that she could use politely, *Mister Something, hello, I'm waiting for Olivia*, and then he would tell her what to call him. She looked from the now-surging washing machine into a blue-and-white-tiled kitchen. A covered stockpot simmered on the stove, chicken soup, she could smell it now, and on a metal kitchen table stood mail, not piles and piles of it, but enough she hoped to give her some information . . . Mr. Philip Horvath, 1134 Arizona Avenue, Santa Monica. *Mr. Horvath, Mr. Horvath, Mr. Horvath*, she repeated and she took up a small plate with two cookies on it, no doubt for Mr. Horvath, and started toward the front room, her backpack still slung across her shoulder. The telephone jangled, startling her, and she halted in a passageway, listening to the man's low voice speaking, words mirthful, then subdued, then consoling, but she didn't attempt to make out their sense. She seized on this bit of extra time. She could see into a dining room on her left. Red camellias floated in a bowl at the center of a glass-topped table, and four silver forks and four silver knives were laid across one end as though they had just been polished. The camellias seemed very still, very meaningful, and then it was silent in the house for what seemed like a very long time.

"Mr. Horvath," she called quietly, "I don't want to scare you." Her tennis shoes were quiet, perhaps too quiet. "Mr. Horvath," she said again, coming onto the patterned rug, her footfalls even quieter. She stood a few feet away from him now, looking down at him, his spoon raised in his hand, his face immobile, tears streaming from his chin. She had never seen such instantaneous tears, nor a man crying. "Mr. Horvath—"

—

"Please stop saying his name. Who are you?"

"I'm a friend of Olivia's."

"Somehow I don't think so," he said weakly.

She was lying to him, and in the face of his sorrow. He hid nothing, attempted to hide nothing, and yet she lied to him, was lying to him. She looked down at the pale blue plate in her left hand. She could see the top masting of a schooner in the porcelain beneath the cookies, the too-perfect, dry-looking store-bought cookies. She wanted to say that she could bake some real cookies, or that she could continue the laundry. She wanted to ask him what his name was, since it seemed that Philip Horvath was not the man before her, his dark gray eyes streaming tears.

"Put those down," he finally said, gesturing his delicate old man's hand at the table beside his chair. He pulled the linen napkin from the tray and dried his face. He wore a black turtleneck and jeans, a thin gold watch. "Would you take this away," he asked, lifting the tray up to her. "Oscar will be mad, but I've lost what little appetite I had."

"What if we had soup together?" she asked him. The tray was still suspended in the air between them, and she hadn't reached for it; she still held the plate of cookies, her backpack across her other shoulder. She wanted to look around the room, to take in her surroundings, but she was afraid to take her eyes from him. She placed the small plate on the table, atop the plain red cover of the book he had been reading. He lowered the tray back onto his lap. "You are certainly not a friend of my niece's," he said sternly, but not meanly. "You are hungry?" he asked.

—

"Yes," she said simply, and she let the strap of her backpack slide down her shoulder and then down her leg until it puddled at the base of his chair within a blue and red geometry in the beautiful rug.

"You have not had your supper?" he asked her.

She stood in her scuffed tennis shoes, her thin dress, her yellow cardigan. She wore a woman's old watch on her wrist, her grandmother's, and she had forgotten to wind it and so the time read eleven o'clock. She covered it, her right hand grasping her left wrist, and the washing machine whirled in the background and she heard again his words, his phrasing, *You have not had your supper. Your supper. Your,* the word *your.* Never before had anyone specifically assigned food to her, *your supper,* as though there were food in the world just for her. The maple syrup this morning had been syrup saved from her father's syrup, his generosity in allowing her some, in not eating all he could have eaten so that there was syrup for her, syrup pried from his share. *Your* supper. She heard the possessive, felt it as some chemical or vitamin now resident and instructive in her veins.

"Serve yourself a bowl," he said. "I'll wait. We can eat together, as you say."

She felt wingéd as she walked to the kitchen, wingéd but attempting with all her might to keep herself grounded, and she looked around the lovely white cupboards on three sides of her, old wooden cupboards, and yet they were hospitable, welcoming. Simple neat stacks of pale blue plates and bowls, and she found a drawer of silverware and a spoon, but then

—

32

she turned to the kitchen table and gently nudged envelopes right and left, looking for another name, and there it was, Mr. Julien Stoke.

"Why are you looking through my mail?" he asked, standing in the doorway, the linen napkin grasped in his hands. "For my name," he then said, answering his own question. "Of course."

"Mr. Julien Stoke."

"Yes."

"I'm sorry."

"I have the feeling you have no choice," he said. "Would that be a good surmise?" As he walked past her, steadily, not like an old man, she wondered if he could hear her heart hammering in her chest. She wasn't afraid of him. She was afraid of him asking her to leave. He lifted the bowl and ladled soup from the pot. It was chunky with white beans and something green and her lungs opened in anticipation, and yet the soup that had been in his bowl wasn't this soup.

"You're eating something different," she said.

"Oscar's infernal white bean chili. I think he thinks that appeals to a gringo. I just want my Campbell's chicken noodle soup. So, he's right on the gringo part. One wants what one wants."

She heard the ease with which he pronounced those words, the complete and utter unassailability of his inflection. *One wants what one wants.* She knew that she would always be amazed, stunned, if she ever got what she wanted. Wanting something and actually having it were two entirely opposed

—

experiences in her life. Until now, she intoned in her head, *until now. Come on*, she urged herself, *it will be different now*, but she didn't really believe this either because she had barely gotten anything, or anywhere, yet. The bus, yes, she'd succeeded in leaving Needles, but with the help of the woman, and Los Angeles, yes, she was here, really truly here, and she had made five dollars hemming the woman's dress, yes, but being thwarted had been so much the mode of her life that she knew to imagine only the worst, only the event or situation furthest from what she really wanted. She'd acknowledged the possibility of her grandmother dying with the excruciating hope that by doing so it would not happen. "Grandmother will die," she said to herself over and over in order to ward it off. "Everyone has to die—Grandmother will die," and her grandmother had lived, her small warm body standing beside her in the kitchen teaching her canning, pear butter and plum jelly and peach preserves, and in her grandmother's bedroom, beside her on her bed, their bodies leaned into each other on the soft mattress, how to smock a little girl's dress and bobbin lace and knitting. "Won't do you much good today, I don't suspect," her grandmother kept saying. "Far different world than the one I grew up in," and then her grandmother would turn and whisper in her ear, "you get yourself out of here," she'd say. "You are better than this. I don't mean you should be prideful. Just you get yourself away from this house, this town. School is the whole world away from this place, bide me."

Then of course her power stopped working. Her grandmother did not wake up. Or she'd never had any power and she knew obliquely that she wasn't making any sense, that she was intemperate, and even thinking of this now, she heated up beneath her skin with shame.

The beginning of difference in her life was tomorrow, her birthday, and she had made this the starting line, the distance she had traveled, and across this line was arrival, arrival that would be marked by a cake, a small cake.

"Do you know if there's a bakery around here?" she asked. "Maybe one close by, and do you know what an opening is?"

"You mean for art?" he asked, turning to her with her bowl of chili. "An art opening?"

"Paintings. I was invited but I don't know what time an opening happens. I forgot to ask, or I didn't know to ask, I mean, I wasn't thinking, or something."

"*Or something*," he said back to her, holding the plate with the bowl of soup on it. He lifted the spoon in his other hand. "Is this what you want," he asked. "A small spoon? Wouldn't you prefer a soup spoon?"

He pulled a drawer open and settled the teaspoon back in and reached out a larger spoon with a wide round bowl. "Soup spoon," he said, holding it up. "Yes? Come."

He walked back into the front room slowly but his hands steady, and she followed, the washing machine whushing loudly behind her. She wanted desperately to hear the machine go into the spin cycle and then whine to a clicking stop. She would then spring from wherever she was in the house and open the washing machine's lid and reach for the twisted towels and sheets and shake them out from their moist torques

—

before placing them in the dryer. She liked putting a house to rights, her grandmother's expression, though in her mind there had been little right about the house she had fled, its cheerless, unwelcoming neatness, its insistent control.

"Sit here," he said to her, this man named Julien Stoke, *sit here* and he pointed at a small upholstered chair near the fireplace. His words were indeed an instruction, but they were not a command, and the difference lit up her mind, and her face flushed with a distinction she had sought but had not been sure she would find. *School is the whole world away from this place, bide me,* she heard her grandmother say to her. She sat down on the small chair within the heavy scent of flowers. How had she not smelled them until this moment? He lowered the plate to her and held out the spoon. The gesture was another instruction that was not a command, a spoon, here! it will help you eat Oscar's infernal white bean chili!

She saw now the long narrow couch along the front window, and above her on the mantel, a vase of tall flowers, and then everywhere on the walls paintings, massive plains of color with lines beneath like darkly healed scars. He would know about art openings, she reasoned; he would tell her what she wanted to understand.

"Taste it," he said to her. He picked up his own tray with his chicken noodle soup on it and settled back into his chair.

"Oscar's infernal white bean chili," she said, venturing a smile. It was thick and substantial in her mouth, but not delicious. It needed a ham hock or bacon, something fat to give it flavor and salt.

"God, don't tell him I called it that. He'll throw you out before I've had a chance to find out who you are—why do you want to know where a bakery is," he asked her, slurping soup from his spoon. "Actually, let's start with your name." He slurped more soup into his mouth, and it seemed to her that now he had an appetite, that now there was some relish evident in the brisk dipping of his spoon and its rise to his mouth. She lifted more and more spoonfuls to her own mouth and felt her stomach expanding with tension and air, and yet she wanted to eat, and was hungry, but the warmth of the soup and its succor ratcheted her into a recognition of what she had done and how far from her quiet mother she was. She understood without articulation that Mr. Julien Stoke allowed her to be calm and at the same time allowed her enough calm to recognize the direness of her running away.

"Let's start with your name," he said again. "Hurry, before Oscar gets back."

"Where is Olivia?" she asked him abruptly, swallowing, hoping there wasn't food on her lips. "Perhaps I could just be Olivia until she comes?" She heard the man in the cowboy boots with the freshly shampooed hair, *Hell, you've come to Lotus Land*, he had said in the cab, and she understood that he meant she could be anyone she wanted to be, anyone she could imagine. But this wasn't exactly why she'd come to Los Angeles. She was already who she was, already the person she had fought to free. She wished she could retract her last words. She wasn't Olivia and she didn't wish to be her, but she could be a more reliable version, she thought, someone who

—

appeared when she said she would, and on time. She needed to ask what time it was, too, to set her watch and to remember to wind it, but Mr. Julien Stoke needed first to call her something. Her words now were solemn and she pronounced them carefully, and without intoning a question: "You could give me a name."

She wanted him to know that naming her was something he would have to do. He could toss her out of his house, yes, but he would have to name the person he was showing the door. In the Bible, Adam had been given the job of naming all the creatures, *And the man gave names to all the cattle, and to the birds of the sky, and to every beast of the field*, and then she thought that maybe she didn't want his name, didn't need it. God had left language up to man, to Adam, but in Genesis God had made sea monsters and every wingéd bird *cattle and creeping things and beasts of the earth* before he made Adam, and so there had been shes before Adam could name them hens and sows and ewes and cows and mares. Maybe instead she just wanted, just needed, to be one of the small unnamed shes of the field and of the sky. Wasn't that a better strategy for the next three years?

"Hmm," he murmured. "I've never named anyone."

But now her heart was not in it and she said without energy, "No children. No pets?"

"Oh, well yes, a dog here or there, but not a girl, never a girl," and then he laughed merrily to himself. *Hmm, never a girl.* But she wasn't laughing, wasn't understanding what he meant. "Okay," he then said, quieting. "You've come from somewhere, and you've come alone," and then he nodded his

—

head at her backpack on the rug, "and that seems about it, yes? One small pink backpack?"

"I'm good around the house, and I can bake—those are from the store, those cookies," and she gestured at the small plate atop his red book. "I could bake you some better ones, fresher at least," she said quickly.

"In Los Angeles, people don't walk into other people's houses and just take up daily chores. That may be the custom of the country wherever you're from, but it will get you taken into police custody here."

She felt anxious, her stomach nervous and distended, a few spoonfuls of soup and then this fretful mounting agony of climbing up into someone's good graces. She could see beneath the chili the masts of the schooner on the porcelain. She did not think her mother would like the pattern of these dishes, but her mother would like that they all matched, and that they were unchipped and shiny. She spoke the one sentence she thought might help her. "You don't know anything about what I've run away from."

Mr. Julien Stoke looked at her carefully, his gray eyes dark and appraising. "This is true. I don't. But it's the year 2013, not Dickensian England where waiflings just show up at the door and somehow become your long-lost relations by novel's close."

"You have a garage," she offered. She didn't know anything about Dickensian England; she didn't wish to be anyone's relation. "Could I stay one night in your garage."

"Of course not," he spoke harshly. Lights flashed through the front window and she heard a car in the driveway, Oscar's car, and she realized the sky had darkened, that evening was falling, and the high whining of the washing machine closing down its cycles emerged too, and Oscar stood in the doorway, eyeing her, eyeing the plate and soupbowl in her hands.

"Friend of Olivia's," Julien Stoke said, his tone of voice playful and curious and amused. She realized that he had heard her speaking with Oscar in the driveway, and neither of them seemed to believe her . . . and yet they didn't seem particularly bothered by the pretense either. "Go on home, now," he said to Oscar. "I'll put the groceries away. You got me some more cans of my soup?" he asked to Oscar's back retreating into the kitchen. Light shone for an instant on Oscar's black hair falling like thick brushstrokes of black enamel paint.

"I like your chili, Oscar," she tried to call out to him, raising the spoon, as though gesturing him back, but she could not be comfortable enough yet to make her voice or this gesture jolly or funny or lilting and it fell flat and dull within the room. When Oscar stood in the archway once again, he was not smiling. He spoke rapidly in Spanish and Julien Stoke answered just as rapidly at first, and then his voice slowed, inflecting a question, and then sped up again and now the words were angry or tense. Oscar started across the room, his arms raised, and she knew what was coming and she grasped harder her plate and bowl, keeping them steady, and she tucked into her body and slid from the chair to the rug, flinching.

The room seemed hollow and quiet for a long time. She felt the heat rising off the soup against the front of her dress, but her fingers gripping the porcelain felt icy and dead. She could smell the wool of the rug. Then she dared to open her eyes, and she could see in her periphery the white canvas of Oscar's high-tops, their red laces. The shoes did not move. Finally she dared look up into their shadowy faces, both sets of eyes quietly studying her. She looked back down at her hands clutching the dishes, and started to unfold, rising and then settling herself back in the small upholstered chair, its fabric rough against the backs of her bare knees. She did not know if the quiet in the room was fortunate or unfortunate, but she knew something had changed and then there was only the thuds of Oscar loading wet towels into the dryer, and the slap of the dryer door pushed home and the back door closing and his car backing out. Headlights flashed once again across the expanse of the living room window, and then she and Mr. Julien Stoke sat in the quiet dimness without speaking.

She dared to eat again, and her spoon clicked against the bowl. Even though her stomach was bloated with tension, she needed to eat what she could. She heard the harshness of his voice *of course not!* when she had asked if she could spend the night in the garage. She tried to finish the chili quickly, tried not to make noise with the spoon scraping across the bowl. He would ask her to depart soon, and she would need to, silently, without fuss, and without leaving any trace that she had ever sat on this small, upholstered chair, within the perfume of flowers she could not name, before a man who seemed for the most part unconcerned with her presence, her situation. She would need to be gone as swiftly and completely as the swiping of a car's headlights across the curtains, the windows—only a

—

small chair sitting empty beneath a canopy of flowers pouring down off the mantel—only this quiet image would remain in the dimness of the room.

She spoke to herself again, assured herself, *It's okay, fine, you didn't expect anything would go well. You had some silly hope for a minute and now that's settled. Get the loquats—ask about the loquats.*

"What do you take me for," he finally asked her.

She settled the spoon back in the bowl, and turned toward him. This was harder, she thought, more intricate. Now it seemed that he didn't just want her gone, but that he wanted her to understand something about who he was, why he was doing what he was doing. Mr. Julien Stoke would not tell her what she was supposed to do, would not direct her; she needed to understand, and just now, in the ever-more-deepening light, she didn't understand what he wanted, what she had done wrong other than be in his house uninvited. What had she taken him for that insulted him so much?

"Do you really think that I would let you sleep in the garage? On what! on cement, or atop boxes? Curled like a cat! Even if you do that curling-up thing really well. Did you really think that Oscar would hit you. Poor man might never recover. Or that I would hit you—or that I would allow anyone to hit you?"

He seemed furious, incensed, and she stammered out apologies and then reached for her knapsack with one hand and held the plate and bowl in the other. "I'll go," she said, rising from the chair. "Thank you—would you let me take some

—

42

loquats from your tree," she then blurted out. "It's why I was in the driveway in the first place—I wanted to ask permission."

"Loquats? That's what you want?" Mr. Julien Stoke said, almost laughing, perhaps trying to. "What on earth?"

But she herself was struggling to understand too. She had done something that insulted both Oscar and Julien Stoke. "And maybe you could tell me what time an opening happens?" she then asked. "An estimate."

"Six," Julien Stoke said quickly, "if you're going for the wine, but the galleries are usually open before that. It's not something you need to be on time for, in fact quite the opposite," he added, almost laughing again, his eyebrows raised up merrily.

"Could I take—"

"Take as many loquats as you like—I hate the things. They taste like earwax."

"Jam. You could make jam with them, you know?"

"Perhaps you could, but I couldn't, or wouldn't. Jam. Can you make jam?" he now asked her seriously, looking up at her. She could barely see his face against the chair back. The paintings, their huge plains of color, seemed to her in this evening light like walls within walls.

"Pies, too. Loquat pie. It's good—you put cinnamon in it, and sometimes loquat jelly, if you cook it long enough, to get the pectin going, you know, sometimes it turns pink. A very light pink jelly. It's pretty," she added, but her voice did not lift on the words.

"What else can you make?" he asked. He reached up and took her plate and bowl and rested them atop his own on his

—

tray. He remained seated, looking up at her. She switched her backpack to her other hand and then reached her arms through the straps. The minute weight of the pack felt good on her shoulders, she was ready to go. She moved a little across the room to stand in some place darker. Almost gone, she thought, he can't see me, and she moved even a little farther against the wall. She didn't speak for a long time; it wasn't going to get her anywhere, and she felt anguished, and so finally she said, "That chili would be much better with some ham in it, or some meat or bacon, something. It has no flavor."

"I'm with you on that one," he said, and then he murmured deeply in his throat, a sound almost from his chest. "Sit down," he said. "Please. I don't want you to leave, but certainly I'm not going to let you sleep in my garage."

"Okay," she said.

"Who taught you to cook?" he asked.

"My—" But she stopped herself. "No one really. I just watch, and then I write it down. I could've baked you some better cookies than those."

"Please," he said, gesturing to the chair, his hand white wings across the room in the dimness. "Sit down." She let her backpack once again slide to the rug, but she still held its straps across her wrist. Then she came back across the room and lowered herself into the chair, its upholstery cool against her thigh, a little rough. She needed different clothing. She knew this now. It was cold this close to the ocean, and outside it would be colder still, and the small comfort sitting in this house provided made her understand what she was up against, what she might

—

not survive unless she figured this out, cajoled her way into his garage, or at least into some cast-off clothing? She'd seen the glazed leather skin of homeless women in Needles, women exposed to the elements, wasn't that the phrase, "exposed to the elements," their faces like baked hams. She wondered, who was Philip Horvath, and where was his clothing? He had died, because otherwise Julien Stoke's tears seemed excessive. But she had never seen a man cry before; maybe she was being unfair; maybe when men cried they cried excessively. "You can bake," Julien Stoke said to her now, "and yet a while back you asked me about a bakery? What's that about? That doesn't seem to make much sense."

"It's my birthday tomorrow." The straps of her backpack now lay across one palm and she perched on the edge of the small chair in the dark. Outside, an occasional car moved down the street, its lights on sometimes, sometimes not, the gradual transitions of evening.

"If I made you a promise, would you tell me everything," he asked.

"It's better if you don't know, isn't it?"

"You mean 'deniability'?"

She nodded her head up and down. The dark felt comfortable, soothing. "Right?" she asked him. "It's a crime?"

"What's a crime? What are you talking about?"

The words had hung in the air of the cab, spoken with disgust and concern by the man in the boots with freshly washed hair. *Harboring a minor.* Maybe if she didn't say the words, maybe then they could not be a crime.

—

"Certainly I'm not going to do anything to you." He had risen, holding the tray before him in both hands, and his voice was tinged with anger again, or perhaps just prickly. He seemed completely steady on his feet and fragile at the same time. She wondered if he was ill. She watched him walk briskly through the door to the kitchen, and then listened to the quiet clatter of dishes as he set them down. "For one thing," he called to her, "I'm old—or OLDER," he amended, amused now. "How about a cup of tea?"

She agreed quickly. "Tea, I'd like that." She could not see him from where she sat by the fireplace, and it was now darker and darker and she looked around the room for lamps or a light switch. There seemed to be plenty, on side tables and behind his chair where he had sat reading. She saw pale columns of candles gathered on a flat dish on a wide expanse of coffee table. Lights from the street bloomed and then faded and bloomed again. She realized there was an entryway behind her and a front door.

"I thought you'd like tea," he said, coming back into the room. "You're freezing, aren't you?" He stood over her. "Is that the only clothing you have? It is, isn't it."

"It's all right," she said. "I'll make do."

"With what?" he asked sternly, the same strict fast intonation he'd used when he'd said *Of course not!* to her staying in the garage. "Make do with what, spiderwebs!"

"If need be. But yes, it would be good to have some warmer clothing."

"*If need be*. Who speaks like that," he said. "You ran away and yet you seem well taken care of, well fed at least."

"Everyone thinks I'm fat," she said, laughing quietly, suddenly relieved to be saying the words. "Fat as a seal, someone called me this morning."

He huffed. "More like baby fat," he said. He held his hands up before his shoulders, *Not to worry, okay. For God's sake, don't flinch when I come near you.* He reached behind her and took something from the mantel, and when a whiff of sulfur infused the air, she realized that it was a box of matches. She had not moved or cowered when he came near her and he seemed pleased by this, though she had also sat stiffly until she understood what he was doing. He leaned over the coffee table and lit the candles, and then straightened, holding the burnt match. He turned and looked at her. "That's not why you left, is it?" he asked her seriously. "Someone called you fat?"

She knew she could say *Of course not*, mimicking his inflection, that she had a choice to be playful in this moment, that it might even win her something, a place to spend the night, warm clothing, food, but she didn't wish to play or be playful. Maybe she did not know how to play, and maybe this would hurt her, that she wasn't willing to be childlike, willing to cut up or clown about. She could not know this of herself in this room flickering with small flames just ignited, this safe cave of a room, its paintings dancing in candlelight now. She could not articulate her resistance as clearly as she might many years hence, that her heart did not rise to play, or fantasy or impossible imaginings. It did not occur to her that mice would suddenly carry her load of firewood, or that a prince would lean down on one knee and make all the bad in the world disappear,

—

or a spaceship hover down and lift her into weird and wonderful light. She felt she knew that magic show of propaganda for what it was, a game of making her concentrate on one thing when something else was happening. Some people might enjoy that hopeful wonder, but she thought it was lying, subterfuge, a kind of cheap carnival of the mind.

She could be called fat seven ways to Sunday, just so she never felt a hand on her body ever again.

"That's stupid, what I just asked. I get it. I'm sorry. Obviously that's not why you left."

"Okay," he said after a time, as though something had been settled between them. "I have three guesses, right," he ventured, working, she could see, to lighten the exchange. "You're either almost fifteen? Almost sixteen? Or almost seventeen? Because if you were already eighteen, or eighteen tomorrow, you wouldn't . . . well, I don't know, but you're hardly eighteen."

"Fifteen tomorrow."

"Lordy," he said.

"I didn't think to go to the opening for the wine," she said. "I wanted to ask the artist why he put the time on his paintings. I saw them on Ocean Avenue, in a window, and they had a time on them, just beneath the artist's signature. Isn't that odd," she asked Mr. Julien Stoke. "Don't you think so?"

"Artists are odd," he said. "That's why they're artists."

"Oh," she said. "Really?"

"Yes, really," he said, sounding exasperated to her. The kettle began to sing and he walked briskly through the archway toward it, and then lights went on in the kitchen and she heard cupboard doors and the twang of a tin opening. What was the promise he was about to make her if she told him "everything?" The candle flames drafted briefly and settled. Why would he make her a promise? He owed her nothing, not even his word, let alone a promise. She heard him settling tea cups and saucers on the tray, and she knew she could rise from the chair and move to the front door. She could lift the chain and slide it the short distance of the brass channel and then let it fall quietly. She could open the heavy wooden door and pass through and turn and pull it snug behind her. The loquat tree would be on her right, and she would see its clusters of yellow fruit in the light from the streetlamp. The fruit would be there tomorrow morning, or later tonight. She could have as many as she liked.

He moved back into the room now, a tray with cups and saucers and a teapot. He set it down on the coffee table and then lowered himself into his chair. His weight made almost no sound, fabric against fabric, but she heard the quiet whine of a spring baffled somewhere deep within the cushion. "We'll let that steep a bit," he said.

"Do you know what time it is?" she asked. "I forgot to wind my watch."

"Whose watch is it?" He looked at her wrist, just as the room grew momentarily light and then darkened again.

"My grandmother's. She died."

"I'm sorry," he said.

"Me too. But she would be happy that I'm here now with you." She watched him pull his head back, consternation in his eyes, his lips twisting. He murmured deeply again, the sound that came up from his chest.

"And she gave you that watch, her watch."

"She wanted me to have it—that's what my mother said."

"Does it work," he asked.

"Sometimes."

"That's convenient."

"I mean, if I remember to wind it."

"Remember to wind it, then," he said, distracted. He held his wrist up into what little light there was. "Five-thirty, I think. You seem not only dropped in," he said, "but dropped in from another era."

"Maybe," she said, not understanding completely. "I don't have a cell phone, if that's what you mean. They could figure out where I was if I did, so that seemed dumb, but people now use their cell phones for telling the time."

"Odd phrase, isn't it?" he asked her. "Telling the time, as though we're telling time anything—anything at all. Your mother worry about you?" he ventured. "Someone who might be hurt by your disappearance?"

She didn't answer. She didn't want to answer, nor did she wish to revisit this issue of her mother, her mother's utter passivity. Was her mother even capable of worry? Was that love? Could that be love? Her mother resided so deeply inside that passivity she could not find who or what her mother was. Of course, she was to be like her mother, to follow in her mother's traces . . . and yet that seemed something so completely of

—

50

her father's insistence that she found it hard to think of it as her mother, or as behavior she should emulate. Wasn't, in some odd way, that passivity really her father's refusal to ask more of himself, his refusal to insist and work at being a better person? He seemed to just allow himself to be vengeful, angry, almost as though he had no control over himself.

"I don't much like electricity," Mr. Julien Stoke said finally, to break the silence. "It's a harsh light. Particularly after Philip died, my eyes couldn't take the light."

"*Don't much like*," she said quietly. "Who speaks like that!?"

"Ha-ha, very funny."

And you shall not lie with a male as one lies with a female; it is an abomination. "I should go," she said. "I've already stayed too long, I know."

"You must suit yourself," he said to her, rising from his chair. He set a cup on a saucer and then poured tea into it, but she had already risen.

"You haven't had your tea," he said, and there it was again, *your tea*, as though there were tea in the world strictly for her, strictly apportioned, hers alone, some part of that pot's contents completely *hers*.

"No, I haven't, have I?" she said, and they both sat back down for the longest time, and then he rose again and handed the warm saucer into her hands, setting it atop the strap of the backpack still in her hands. She could not see that he was an abomination, but she realized she did not know what abomination meant, either. Always she had thought she did know, the word's indwelling force, the disgust. But he just seemed old and sad and rather basic, someone whose laundry was drying in another room and whose dishes sat on the countertop in the kitchen, needing to be washed. Still, she could not stay to do these small chores, even if he allowed her to, she could not be here.

DOGS

The dogs had always come to her across a room.

Their serious eyes in their uplifted faces, their swift, slapping tails against her legs.

Often she felt bad about herself, dissenting. *The elevator didn't go to the top floor,* she'd murmur, or *Not the sharpest tool in the shed, Not painful on the eyes, but no one would linger, either. No one,* she'd say to herself, and yet she'd be pleased, too, by her ease within anonymity. She was corps de ballet, and no one but her mother could distinguish her out of a line-up, and that was how it was supposed to be, how she loved her dancing to be, synchronous and precise, one of a dozen elegant arms, one of a dozen pale pink legs in arabesque, a piece of the perfection but not the perfection itself.

But the dogs, they found her, singled her out, as they had now at her parents' party, her party really, hers and Ben's, their engagement. The dogs now swarmed about her ankles and calves, the dogs who had made a difference to her always, their primal affection from somewhere so deep and creatural it was unassailable, better, purer, more substantial than any human evaluation.

She knew her gratitude was out-sized, a bit absurd. Of course. But she relished it anyway, an appraisal utterly and completely about her, about her heart, not about who her father was, or about this house in Hancock Park where she'd grown up—not about the prima ballerina people thought she could have been. She held this appraisal of the dogs close to her, precious, her canine teachers, she mused, they thought well of her, against all odds within her world, the dogs came to her, gave her their highest marks.

And now Teddy and Victoria, their brisk efficient corgi selves, stood at either side of her, this celebration of her engagement in full throttle, and Teddy very fussed. Teddy growled, and though it could barely be heard above the ebulliently confident laughter of her parents' friends, above the Bill Evans piano being played in the next room, Teddy growled. Later, there would be a toast, her father lifting a glass, hailing the attention of the room, presenting his daughter and her fiancé, "remember Little Ben Carmichael" her father would be saying, "and now we need to convince him to make a lateral down here to the firm where he should be." There would be laughter and hear-hears. She and Ben would stand beside the engagement cake with its intricate vining of English ivy, ivy for fidelity, her mother said, the variegated lobed leaves shaped from sugar paste, and here and there stephanotis blossoms so faithfully recreated she could only tell they were paste because they did not smell of the lovely perfume of stephanotis. But now, the three of them, she and the two corgis, stood in the corner of the dining room, gazing out through the opened French doors onto the enclosed courtyard. Everywhere her parents' friends.

Too many sheep, hmm? she said to Teddy, looking down at his surprising blue-merle coat, at his poised, avid ears. *Whatta ya gonna do, Teddy-O, whatta ya gonna do? Ya can't herd em all into one room.*

Teddy twisted his thickly furred neck, his imperious muzzle, and looked up at her briefly. He then turned back to this predicament, drunken sheep everywhere. She had watched him once work the outside perimeter of one of her parents' parties, both Teddy and Victoria moving in tandem, people slowly and without knowing it being moved from the courtyard up the broad stairs and into the dining room until Teddy had succeeded at containment and her mother had finally looked up, people crushing at her elbows, and said *What the hell?* laughing but not amused. "Teddy, stop that!"

Now a server in black pants and white shirt moved sinuously about the room proffering his tray of hors d'oeuvres, and then he stood near enough that she could smell him, his peppery scent, peppery she allowed, and then she thought *rank, he smells rank.* Teddy's growl mounted and Victoria began now, too.

"They were okay with me before," said the server, looking at her, then looking farther down at the dogs.

"Teddy, Victoria, it's okay. Stop it. This man is just trying to make sure we have cheese puffs."

"They're protective of you," he said, laughing, his hazel eyes a little wide and loose. He was no doubt high on something, and then she knew, cocaine, which she hadn't smelled for a few years really, its distinct pharmaceutical smell, and yet his eyes didn't match cocaine. New drugs—God knows what he was on, but she could barely stand his smell, and she plucked

—

two cheese puffs off his tray, thanked him and gestured him on. She could act the young woman of privilege if she had to, and yet cowling over her like dark clouds was a formation of ferocious shame. She had meant her hand waving him on to be humorous, to say "move along now," an extension of the dogs, but she knew it appeared cool and instructional. She admired kind people, and this server had been good-natured and obliging earlier, helping to set up the bar, dragging in bags of ice so the party could "go full bore when the bartender arrives." He'd then unfolded a bar towel and carefully wiped his hands and then turned to her mother and said, "May I," indicating her linen dress half zipped up. "You're a keeper," her mother had said.

Now, both Teddy and Victoria's muzzles were pointed up at her, waiting. They knew cheese puffs with their names on them. They were corgis.

"They're too hot," she said, smelling the toasted sprinkle of parmesan cheese across the puff-pastry tops. "You shouldn't be eating them anyway—you're both tubby." Teddy and Victoria turned their attention back to the party, as though dismissive of her comment, as though to say, *Of course we're tubby. We're born like this. We're corgies!* "Too smart for your own good," she said down at them, "and I am too much dog now for mine," she murmured. A few feet away two men stood in dark business suits, talking quietly, and she could smell both of them, a day's mild sweat beneath strong cologne. She'd known these men since she was a small child, attorneys in her father's firm, partners, and now in the firm a very modest showing of young women associates, but these constantly in flux and gone from the letterhead soon enough. She knew the story that wasn't a story of the young associate who played golf, and who at a firm retreat had hit a ball off the tee so disastrously that she'd said loud enough for all to hear "Fuck me," and she was gone within a few months. Of course those things were never the reasons, and yet they were tincture, quiet reservation—these got easily, pervasively on a reputation and moved about unchecked; no performance or CV contained them, countermanded them. She realized she was thinking about something akin to smell, to how smell could work a room.

She felt the cold tip of Victoria's nose at her ankle. "What?" she said. "Oh." It was Ben, striding toward them, shaking hands as he came, leaning down to plant chaste kisses. He was so dear, she thought, so easy with this show, or at least good at pretending he was, and he'd be at her side soon enough, some funny, breezy comment just for her small ear, "Holy cock-sucking Gott im Himmel," he'd whisper in his comedic German. "Scheisserei—rye whiskey, yes, thank you very much! Bring on the rye!" And she'd be laughing instantly, freely, happy he was there finally, her hand tucking beneath his elbow, her cheek against his shoulder, and she could not stand his smell. She'd hold her other hand across her face as though covering her laughter, pretending to behave herself, but she'd be blocking her nose from his scent, willing herself not to gag, her stomach not to twist in revulsion. Teddy and Victoria growled now, almost barking, and moved out into the dining room and against Ben's dark pants. Ben held his hands up, *I sur-*

render, looking down at them. He stood three yards away, his eyes imploring her *call these fucking dogs off*, and just then the partners turned and held their hands out to Ben, congratulating him, all the dark-suited male arms, and she had a moment to think.

She knew what it was. She had taken the pill for ten years, since she was fifteen, the wee white pill of contraception that kept her body from telling stories on her, from broadcasting her sex life, the wee white pill that kept her from being punished for this one night, and that night, and oh *that night!* too, in Copenhagen, what a colossal mistake *he* had been, but then just a year ago Ben stood in dim light at the foot of the stage entrance stairs, talking quietly to Gus. "She'll be down," Gus was saying, "and she is one sweet person," and then they both looked up to see her standing on the landing, her face still glistening with sweat, the freezer bag of ice for her left knee dripping in her hand.

"Who you talking up now, Gus?" she asked, clomping inelegantly down the stairs, her legs exhausted and wobbly. She was halfway down the stairs, and then all the way down and twisting slightly past them both and then walking on the street, and looking back. "It's got to be short for Asparagus, Gus. No one named you Augustus twenty years ago, believe me, you had hippie commune parents who liked their pee to smell."

"Yeah, yeah," he said laughing, and then, "Hey, hold up, this here gentleman is here to see you and he's been waiting a bit."

No, she'd thought, please no. She was corps de ballet, and barely even that now that her knee was blown. She wasn't

—

who people waited at the artists' entrance to fall all over, their faces bright and nervous above a clutch of flowers. She was a perfectly, anonymously sized dancer amid a lake of perfectly, anonymously pale pink swans, or she was one of twenty white-veiled Wilis dancing through the forest in the moonlight. Who could possibly have sat forward—even in an orchestra seat—and picked her out?

She could see ahead of her down the sidewalk to Van Ness Avenue and its river of cars. She could see reticulated buses moving along within the river of cars, bright-lit undulant tubes full of people going home. She had raised her head and looked farther, looked all the way across Van Ness Avenue to the lighted façade of the public library where just that day a man had picked up a chair and brought it down upon the head of another man. *Unprovoked*, the news kept saying, *police are still trying to determine why a man attacked another man in San Francisco's Main Library today.* But newscasters delivered those words without the inflection of a question, and being the child of an attorney, she understood that reasons didn't really matter all that much. The attack, this extreme physicalization, was the news, and we all walked around with a load of why all of the time . . . and it wasn't yet news. Most of us wouldn't allow it to be, she thought, we kept ourselves close, we didn't strike out.

She had slowly turned back to Gus and to whomever this other man was waiting for her. She was not used to turning without a spot to fix her balance, and so her eyes held to the huge golden dome of City Hall . . . and then her eyes didn't and the War Memorial Opera House loomed beside her.

—

"Friend of your father's," Gus called down the sidewalk, "or the son of a friend of your father's. You never said your daddy was an attorney at law," Gus said as she neared, pronouncing the words with mock respect. "You're the child of warmth and security, aren't you."

Gus liked this young man who stood in a contemporary suit, the pants too short, the jacket too snug. Gus liked him— otherwise Gus would not be talking like this, beckoning her back, teasing her, helping the guy, and this meant something to her, that Gus liked him, and she had relaxed. It hadn't changed the fact that she wasn't showered and that she held a dripping bag of ice for her knee, and it hadn't changed the fact that all she wanted was her knee frozen to numbness on the bus and then her great claw-footed bathtub with a book for the rest of the night.

"What?" she had said. "What?" and her tone was a little drastic, a little catastrophic. "My father doesn't really *have* any friends."

Gus laughed. "Yeah, well, no matter, they got some sons and this is one of them. Ben. And Ben," Gus said, turning to him, "she needs to ice her knee, so whatever you do, make sure she gets that cold laid down."

"Car," this man named Ben said, "I've got one. I'll take you home. Carmichael, that's my dad. Thomas Carmichael."

Of course she knew who Thomas Carmichael was, and now she even knew who this man was, living mostly at his mother's in Santa Rosa, the child from Carmichael's first marriage, the child before the two children of his wealthy dotage in Los

—

Angeles. "Ben, wow, hi," she had said sincerely, and then they were off, Ben taking the bag of ice from her and walking her down the street to his car, a Jeep, in the loading zone, its hazards blinking. He pulled the flimsy door open, and after he'd helped her up into the seat and she'd settled, he leaned in and said, "Which knee?" His face had been turned toward her, and he smiled, and she could see the dark circles beneath his vibrant eyes, the gentle slump of his cheeks. He smelled of lawyering, long, long days of mental work, the remnants of an expensive cologne, elegant food, exhaustion. She knew this smell, understood it, understood its toll. He needed her, she could see this. She was a kind of homecoming for him, a part of something he'd not lived around as a child other than vicariously, the law firm, its events and parties, its endless supply of tickets to ballgames and tennis matches and movie premiers, and maybe he wanted to have been a part of that life in Southern California, but maybe he didn't want it either? Maybe he hadn't missed a thing? She hadn't lived around it for years now. She had become something entirely impractical, and far more difficult, a classical ballet dancer. But she understood immediately that he was struggling. What could make all of this work worth it to him? He knew she understood, his tired face looking down at her in the cab of the Jeep. "Which knee?" he asked. "I don't want to tangle with Gus. He looks out for you. Larkin Street, right? Russian Hill?" and as Ben shifted in and out of second and third gears on the steep San Francisco streets, he asked her questions. How was it to grow up in L.A.? Your father won that case, right? How is he? Of course I went to law school, Ben

—

had sighed, turning the ignition off in front of her apartment building. "How else could I tease a little attention from my old man! It's not like I could have chosen the other knee!" And so from that evening forward "Which knee?" became code for "Where does it hurt?" Or code for "Get it right or there'll be a big ta-doo." It was getting the right knee to make their parents happy, choosing the knee that garnered the requisite points, or even purposefully getting the wrong knee in order to make a stand, "Which knee?" meaning which battle are we going to choose here? "Which knee?" one would say to the other and they'd crack up laughing, they'd been that instantly close for months and months, the tremendous easefulness of a past that needed no explaining, no defense or criticism, no attention unless they chose to go there.

What about getting married? Ben asked, sitting across from her one late night after a performance, a small table that looked out onto Columbus Avenue in North Beach. On a white plate between them floated a rum baba, its candied citron glistening.

"Both knees," he said to her. "With you there's no trauma, no lesser of two evils to choose, no road not taken—you just seem like freedom to me, wide open space. We'll make of it what we will. Okay," he said, gazing at her across the table in the quiet flicker of candleflame, *okay?* he implored.

Cool blue moonlight had lit the stage that evening, and the girls, all in gossamer blue gowns, had watched as the Waltz Girl was carried off atop the shoulders of the few male dancers in *Serenade*. Waltz Girl's hair cascaded down her arched back, it, too, glowing in the moonlight, the girls all watching her be carried off, the corps de ballet's ballet she thought to herself now at the table, the ballet in which the steps were all quicker, more exciting, everything bigger, the corps allowed to dance, to be individual, but tonight, the piqué turns in circle, the peeling off of each of them, and her knee, the menisci each time grinding, though she had always been a dancer well turned out from the hip, her body open within its compactness, a perfect dancer for Balanchine, capable of doing everything bigger, but her dancing was almost over and the X-rays like the cool blue moonlight showed it.

In the restaurant on Columbus Avenue, she'd picked up her fork, tipped it into the macerated cake. "Okay," she said quietly to Ben, *okay.*

But then her bleeding, spotting here and there, not calendered as menstrual bleeding is when you're on the pill, and she'd stopped taking it a month ago, happily, this new life she had embarked on deserved a new unalloyed self and now they were all here, in her parents' home, all waiting to wish Ben and her their most heartfelt good wishes for an excellent married life. Ben was winking at her across *the damn dogs*, his eyes happy and at once resigned, *these damn dogs would never accept him, but she had!* He could live with that.

But there was such a thing as chemistry, and the pill had interrrupted it. Ovulation, of course, but some other interruption or shield, too. And now her sense of smell was back and certain men smelled very strongly to her, unpleasantly, which would be fine if one of those men weren't the man

—

she was engaged to be married to. Whatever the mechanism, whatever the science, her body was saying no, and perhaps her mind was, too, but where the rational resided in all of this, she did not know. She would normally equate the science with the rational, but if she said to her gynecologist, "Since I've stopped taking the pill, I can't stand to be in the same room with my fiancé," she didn't think he'd respond very well, the rationalist, the scientist, and he was already too good at assigning the psychological, the psychiatric, and yet there was some science here that had caused this. The palm reader or fortune-teller would nod her large wise head and say, "Of course, of course, you cannot marry him, your body is telling you this." She would lift her hands, rings on all the fingers, a charlatan in every detail, and she would say, "Listen to your body, listen to your heart."

Up until a month ago their lovemaking had been quiet, charged, that, too, a homecoming, an immediate ease, and Ben had been funny, too, "Hey, great, with a delicate knee I'm always on top. Way I like it!" he joked as he turned her over onto his chest and her compact muscled body softened across him, and she seemed to resolve deep down into his chest. Her face rested within that crevasse between clavicle and chin, and he smelled so good to her, and it was fine, lovely, comfort beyond measure, even his thigh a pillow to her bad knee . . . and then, a month ago, it wasn't fine, and she thought she was sick, the flu, or maybe just jitters, all Ben's fault, all the visibility of announcements and then this engagement party and her desire to operate as a gear amid many gears somehow put aside. But she was being unfair, wildly unfair. She had signed on for all of this, happily, even giddily, Ben's joy in caring for her deepening every day, she his reason for work, she, and now this proposed life together, this better reason for his working so hard, and she had barely seen Ben in the last month, his billable hours near humanly impossible. "I'm the one sane kid on a playground full of bullies," he said of working with partners, but she had been grateful he was gone, the apartment they now shared, quiet, smelling of flowers and Japanese incense, the air off the bay if she opened the windows.

Teddy and Victoria accompanied her out into the courtyard— low, thick-bodied sentries at her side—and she found it inter- esting that people did not stop her, as they stopped Ben, or her parents, that she walked through her own engagement party barely a distinct presence. Corps de ballet, she thought, some- thing she'd been good at, being an attendant, being background, ensemble support, atmosphere, a swan amid swans on a lake, a spirit amid spirits in a forest. She saw people looking, comment- ing, even smiling, but no one approached her or stopped her. They smelled her doubt, she thought, they smelled that this pro- posed marriage might not happen. Engaged but not committed. Could she bring herself to stand outside the expectations and call this production off? Maybe only Teddy and Victoria could under- stand, or not understand, but . . . and she stumbled about in her mind looking for the word or phrase . . . maybe only Teddy and Victoria could truly know. It was instinct and they could sense the smells were all awry.

Bougainvilleas grew in the courtyard, their thick old canes rising against the high stone walls. She had grown up in this house, in this garden. She had used the low brick wall around the roses as a barre for exercises, ports de bras. She had practiced pas de bourrée and pas de chat across these flagstones. The courtyard and its plantings looked like the past to her, but now they seemed like a very distant past, a senescence in the old canes and in the moss so deeply comfortable going about its greening. She knelt down to feed Teddy and Victoria each a cheese puff, but their rich avid faces were intent on their plans. They were working dogs, herders—they knew how to contain the herd, not to be a part of it. The dogs smelled good to her, familiar, their silky coats recently bathed. They paid her no mind. She saw the intricate fretwork of her dress against the flagstones, the cheese puffs in her out-stretched hands, untouched.

She stood up, her knee edgy, mean . . . she projected herself into middle age, unmarried, alone, walking through a dog shelter. She would be wanting companionship, a dog, someone to love and to love her, but none of the dogs even looked up at her through their metal cages, and none moved toward her in the open enclosures, or wagged their tails. She hunkered down, she held her hand out, she spoke to the dogs with inflection, with that excited lilt of the voice. She was good with dogs—dogs loved her! But the Norwich terrier mix looked elsewhere, the Labrador's tail remained still.

The officious kindly women who ran the shelter would say that perhaps she should come back, that they didn't feel any of these dogs were right for her and yet they would have walked her purposefully to a black dog curled up and sleeping on a striped pad. "Seven years old, but such a sweet dog!" and they'd already done the implants, already replaced her missing teeth, "she has years in her yet!" but the old spaniel would not raise her head.

We need to see that a dog responds to you, they would then say, walking her out, but they wouldn't be saying it, of course. They wouldn't need to say it. She would have had her time and it was past.

—

SHE

The alley suddenly filled with the concussive revving of a motorcycle without its muffler, and after this loudness the whine of a garage door rising up. In the light of the garage-door mechanism, a man sat astride his bike, his mouth slightly open, a cigarette floating on his lower lip. She supposed that saliva held it there. He watched her, his lighter in his hands, not quite to the cigarette tip, just stayed in the air before his tilted face, looking at her as she made her way in and out and around the immaculate garbage bins, not stopping, moving, and not moving too, her eyes steady, wary, holding him, *Don't look at me, don't come near me.* Then his hands did move, the lighter flame igniting, then shut out, the cigarette tip starting to glow. He pulled the front of his leather jacket open and tucked his lighter inside the breast pocket. He inhaled from his cigarette and then blew smoke out the right side of his mouth past it. In the light, his black hair shone, and she could see it pulled into a long tail down his back. He raised his chin, acknowledging her, and something about this gesture amused her, his face imperious, completely without fear. She responded with her right hand, lifted at her side into a short wave, something he did not even perhaps see as she continued down the alley, past the garage now. His gloves lay across the gas tank, but he didn't put them on and instead sat astride his motorcycle smoking, waiting as she passed. Both of his hands were on the

—

grips, one twisting the throttle, the noise deafening and then becoming quiet and then deafening again as he twisted. His face schooled her, showed her a stance, an attitude of impassive power. He smoked without touching his cigarette, and she wondered what he did for a living that he smoked without using his hands.

It was something she'd once seen a car mechanic do, the cigarette hanging from his lips, moving as he turned the piston in his hands, telling her father it was cracked. "Couple days maybe, but it's not going to last long," the mechanic had said, the words emerging from his mouth in billows of smoke. She understood that the piston he held was not from her father's car, but rather a blown piston the mechanic kept to show people what he meant by piston. He had said as much. She watched his oiled hands circling the rings on the cylinder, and she watched the fury collecting in her father's shoulders, the world of mishaps having its way with him, his careful, staunch life.

"You can't fix it?" she ventured to say.

She remembered her father laughing, looking across her head at the mechanic, seeking male fellowship. "The wife, her mother, this one, they all think a little thread and a needle— that's all it takes."

"I didn't say that," she said. "And I don't think that."

"Who are you to say anything at all," her father spoke quietly, "let alone deny what you said or did not say."

The mechanic looked down at her, the perception in his eyes floating out to her over his flat cheeks, his long cigarette. He pursed his lips tighter around the cigarette,

—

speaking to her, his distaste of her father. "This is essentially a pressure chamber," he said to her, "and when it's cracked, that pressure can't build up."

"If I wanted her to understand the workings of an internal combustion engine, I'd tell her myself."

"It's just that I'm a reliable source for that information," the mechanic had said, laughing, teasing her father. "You don't seem to know jack until I explain it to you."

Jack. Know jack. You don't seem to know jack. That word still snapped in her head, *jack*, a tiny click of insight she needed to have, information from the outside, *And if they desire to learn anything, let them ask their own husbands at home, for it is improper for a woman to speak in church.* And she had learned to intone in her head *jack, he doesn't know jack, he doesn't know jack.* No wonder her father distrusted anything beyond their house and the church building, though he had been the one to choose the hot dusty streets of Needles, this small town in the high desert that looked like the Holy Land, he said, the land that Jesus had walked in his simple sandals.

She moved swiftly now, almost to the street, the light of the open garage behind her. In her periphery vision she saw the man's boot stomping down, then the garage door descending, whining into a sweeping snugness, the sound of rubber weather-proofing against concrete. The motorcycle moved down the alley and when she turned, he was a huge bug bearing down on her, and then flying past, his long tail of black hair hanging out the back of his helmet. She hadn't seen him put the helmet on, or what he had done with his cigarette, but turning now completely and looking farther up the alley, she saw its small glow on the asphalt, as though it summoned her. She had never smoked anything and she thought to retrieve this cigarette and to try lifting it to her mouth and inhaling, some fascinating sophistication in this, in the reveal of the wrist, pale and narrow and flashing, but it was merely a thought. She turned back to the street and watched the motorcyclist turn at the corner and disappear in a roar, and then she retraced her steps toward this quiet red ember, and once there, she moved the toe of her tennis shoe down atop it and smashed it out. Just as quickly she regretted having done this, as though there had been some lively possibility here and she'd smothered it, this delicious smell in the chilly evening air. She realized she was sad, deeply sad, her hard father who meant so much righteousness and truth, and her good mother whose reticence and submission worked itself to a desperate exhaustion within which her mother receded further and further. Her parents were in Needles, in their shabby clean house, and she was in Los Angeles, and she was cold and she had to admit that she had never been cold before, never cold without the possibility of warmth, and she was scared and she hadn't been scared today before now, standing in the center of an alley, resolute, still resolute, yes, but scared, too. She hadn't bargained on that, being scared, being stymied, stilled into quandary, and then there were cars in the alley and garages opening magically and lights coming on and children complaining, and she knew that all would go on without her, that it did not matter what or who she was as she stood tucked closely against a garden gate. She was one more girl flung off the swirling wheel. Remember, she said to herself. Her disappearance hardly registered, and this was her solace, her ticket, and her sadness, *who are you to say anything at all.* Nobody, she said to herself, remember, nobody, this great release into anonymity, and the only purchase she had, that she was now nobody.

Or she was someone new, someone unrecognizable to anyone she had ever known, someone knowable only to those she was about to meet, or had already met today, the tall man in his beautiful boots who had let her ride in his taxi, and Julien Stoke, and Oscar, and the woman in the art gallery whose skirt she had hemmed. She had dared to bolt, to strike out, to run for her life. She felt the intense shame of her immodesty heating her. What vanity, and she knew this, how bold and shameful it was, her insistence on being something other than what her father wished her. She was frozen against this metal gate, her skin taut and anxious, and she felt scolding shame, but she had not been allowed to see her grandmother, to accompany her to wherever they had taken her. She didn't think her grandmother was buried in Riverview Cemetery beneath a cottonwood tree. This possibility had been discussed and the cemetery was owned by the city, and inexpensive, but there was no money for even the simplest coffin allowed by law, and her father had scoffed, repeating the phrase *allowed by law*, as though the city's laws were rules made up by children that could have nothing to do with him. But her father couldn't burn his mother-in-law's remains either, as she was Christian—even if not his kind of Christian—and she didn't deserve the Devil's flame even if she was a *weak woman weighed down with sins, led on by various impulses.* Where was her grandmother now? Where was her body that she was not to care about, her body that was just a vessel, a conveyance of her soul. Dead, of course, she knew her grandmother had died, peacefully in her sleep in her bedroom in their house. That's what her mother kept saying, "peacefully in her sleep," but something told her differently, and her father had insisted she not enter her grandmother's room, that she must stay at the kitchen table. He kept asking her to remember that *we do not walk according to the flesh, but according to the Spirit,* yes, she said, yes, *according to the Spirit,* but I want to see her, to say goodbye to her, and she had pleaded with her father, reaching out to him, and he had taken both of her hands in the metal grasp of his fingers and directed her to sit down, to pray, to help them all in this moment of need. She listened to her parents going in and out of her grandmother's bedroom, the door handle being twisted, rattling, and then the sweep against the carpet as the door closed and opened and closed again. She heard her father's voice muted behind the door giving her mother instructions. Then she heard him ask loudly, "Can't they be washed?"

She had sat at the table and looked around the kitchen, looked at the salt and pepper shakers, a rooster and a chicken, both chipped, and an amber seam running through the white ceramic feathers of the chicken glued back together. She saw the skillets on the stove, mottled with use no mat-

—

ter how clean, and the warped aluminum pan her mother boiled eggs in, and then she rose from her chair and pulled her grandmother's recipe card from the plastic clip on the refrigerator. Queen of Muffins. She had the recipe now with her in the black wallet in her backpack, and someday she would fork the sugar into the butter, the way her grandmother did, and the one egg, and then as few strokes as possible to fold in the silky flour. They were perfect, simple muffins that baked up into toasted ridges as though crowned with gold. *We do not walk according to the flesh*, and so what had her parents done with her grandmother's body, her hands so old and smooth, and her grandmother's long fine hair that her grandmother twisted up and pinned atop her head so quickly it was like a flower suddenly in bloom! "Let me try," she used to exclaim, "let me put your hair up," and she'd taken the long hairpins and set them down studiously across the bed, "preparation as careful as a surgeon," her grandmother teased her. "I think it's just more natural—you kind of sweep it up and don't think too much about it. You're going about it a little too concertedly." Then her grandmother would lean across the groaning bed and kiss her cheek, and was it her grandmother's breath or the Florida Water she always wore that swept into her ear, "You get away from here," away from here, away from here? Perhaps there had been a first time her grandmother had whispered this, a time in which she'd heard the words newly spoken, her brain deciphering them, "get away," what could that mean? and "here," what was meant by "here?" This house, or "here" as in Needles? But she cannot remember a first time; she cannot remember ever not feeling her grandmother's breath across her ear or a time in which she could not smell her grandmother, the Florida Water she wore in defiance of her son-in-law, the words and the cologne inextricable, the shell of her ear awash in her grandmother's words, her grandmother's breath, her grandmother's scent.

The masked wrestler in the droopy spandex tights with the full black merkin scrapes goopy feces from his rear and tosses it indiscriminately at the referees, at fellow masked wrestlers, at the announcers high up above the stage. "Ooh," the crowd groans ecstatically, lifting drinks in the air. The wrestler wipes himself down with a rag, holds the rag to a downed referee's face, and then drags it across the referee's shirt, the black and white stripes being soiled, uproarious pleasure, that referee being smeared with shit is every manager, every fascist department chair, every boss or unreasonable parent.

The crowd is fucking entranced!

She's with beautiful young women, friends, most of them lesbian, professional, their faces in the penumbra of performance lighting completely open and laughing. It's a birthday celebration, and yet somehow the straight faces she observes, including perhaps her own, look distinctly different in the scrim of reservation across their features and smiles, their cloaked, watchful eyes? *This is really out there!*

Li'l Chicken, five feet or shorter, is packing enough genitalia in his yellow briefs to outfit about six Y chromosomes, and so

"All his?" gets shouted wondrously back and forth as he's tossed about by Mini Shamu. Then Li'l Chicken does some of his own tossing, the great bustle of pale yellow chick fluff feathering out from his shapely ass, feathering the air as he flies here, there, up onto the turnbuckles padded in fuchsia pink, off the turnbuckles, an all-out diving body slam onto Shamu, the springs beneath the wrestling ring rattling loudly, chains and bolts and squeaky screws, a castle keep—

"*Sexo y violencia!* masked Mexican Wrestling and saucy striptease. L.A.'s own carnaval," though it is past Mardi Gras, past Carnival. It is the fourth of May, 2012, and it is thirty-three days past Lent, the season of giving it all up, the season of penitence, but she is not much past anything she can get beyond.

That's what death does, she knows now, is to recontrive the calendar, make it one you've never seen before, never moved within. There is this event, his death, and you keep being returned to it, a Möbius strip of time that enfolds you and then lets you emerge, lets you breathe, and then folds you under again—

But she's having a fabulous time. Marisa has brought them all here for her birthday, has presented everyone with a card, letterset, with a sentence, and hers is Jonathan Swift, "No wise man ever wished to be younger," and its envelope contains a press-on mustachio, too—there's one in everyone's envelope—

—

and she's wearing a long candy-colored coat and jeans and boots and several strands of pearls and amethyst beads . . . and a mustache, and she is out for the evening and happy—

—and now on stage all in black spandex but with long white spines down the back of his head and around his waist is Chupacabra throwing one of the Crazy Chickens out into the crowd and beer is flying in great foamy arches, and the yellow-jacketed bouncers are there quickly and holding wildly happy people back from being hurt by flying masked wrestlers, but she can see that people have chosen to stand in certain places for the mosh pit action, wrestlers being flung and then other wrestlers flying out over the ropes to land like human mattresses atop the pile. There's a flurry of yellow jackets and screaming people and laughter and the music is blaring and the huge chandelier of the Mayan Theatre, an Aztec calendar stone, glows high above them in this fantastic Mayan Revival movie palace built in downtown Los Angeles in 1927.

Earlier, driving to the Mayan Theatre down Pico Boulevard, rush hour fizzling, but enough traffic nonetheless, she had seen a black man standing on the curb just past La Cienega, both arms raised high in the air, hailing drivers happily, his meaty purple penis erect from his fly and urinating in a lovely Seventeenth-Century-Formal-Garden-Fountain-with-Pissing-Putti arc.

—

OUT

The evening is on, she had laughed, *I am out on the town.*

In her rearview mirror, the crystal arc of urine against the twilight sky, *For how long can he go?* she wondered. How long before the cops pulled his arms down and bound them behind his back? They wouldn't be kind, but maybe, if the cops were watching, as she still was, they'd be impressed.

How will that work, she wondered? Would the cops make him tuck himself in before they cuffed him, and if the arc of his urine was still perfect against the twilight sky, would they have to wait, seething no doubt though maybe they'd be laughing, probably not, but maybe? Maybe they'd wonder, too, "How long can he go?" and they'd wait and then have him tuck his penis into his shorts and then cuff him? Would they send him on his way, because jailing him for indecent exposure was yet more paperwork and cost to the taxpayer and really no facilities for mental health anyway and so why bother?

She's wanting to have a good time tonight, needs to have a good time, but she thinks these thoughts, wonders also how many times he might have been picked up for indecent exposure. She knows if this is his third arrest, it's three strikes, he's out, or in, and perhaps for a long time, and no mental health care there, either, in prison, as care of a mind is too expensive for a profit margin, too amorphous, unending. More and more cuts to public education everyday.

—

In her rearview, cars and more cars, then the hulk of a truck and she can't see him any longer.

Farther along on Pico, she had seen the dark branches of the jacaranda trees purpling into bloom, and it is the season of star jasmine and the air is sweet with its flower.

She's just crossing Fairfax and she smells sausages cooking on a griddle in the parking lot of the lavanderia and people are gathered, waiting, and the man with his small cart is taking money as he turns onions and peppers and sausages with an avid, able dexterity.

Appetite, she thinks, people waiting for sausages, appetite in the deft twisting and wielding of the huge spatula across the griddle, and within the Mayan Theatre, looking out across the open floor, appetite in the faces penumbraed by the lights from the stage.

They are watching a lithe muscular femininity, a set of particularly fine narrow shoulders set above sinewy calves in stiletto heels, and when the bustier comes off and this beauty is a young man, such tremendous satisfaction of surprise, the surprise a kind of relief at the explanation of this beauty.

. . . but what does that mean, that relief, that sense of resolution that this beauty is a man? What niggling question got answered?

—

Outside, high above in the evening sky, are the silhouettes of palm trees. A skyline of dark pineapples. Pine Apples, symbol of hospitality, welcome, the pineapples once impaled upon gate posts, a return from exotic places—which meant also, a return from places of forbidden admixtures, Christopher Columbus, the Carib. Women with women, men with men. Brave New World.

Even earlier, before the drive to the Mayan down Pico, she'd finished reading a novel, *House Made of Dawn*. There is a character, a fleshy white woman who laughs too easily, Milly, a social worker in 1952 Los Angeles, whose cases are Kiowa Indian men, drunkards and convicts, and the novel is written by a Kiowa Indian man who at the time of publication is an associate professor of English at UC Berkeley. His character Abel, a young Kiowa, says of Milly: "There was no shyness in her. She had looked him squarely in the eye, had spoken up and laughed—she was always laughing—from the very first. Easy laughter was wrong in a woman, dangerous and wrong."

She is a not particularly fleshy white woman laughing, surrounded by wild, exuberant laughter, and she is struck by the idea of laughing women being dangerous—struck by the idea that laughing lesbian women are perhaps even more dangerous.

But no one has come out for anything but a good time; no one has come thinking to keep it all in. No one has walked

from the parking lots along Hill Street, past the parking attendants waving their lighted batons, past the tricked-out low rid-
ers parked in front of the theater jumping and heaving on their
hydraulic suspensions, *banda* blaring from their radios—no
one has walked past all this not wanting the release of carnival.
There is a call and response repeated every few minutes. When
the announcers yell *"Lucha,"* the entire open floor of the Mayan
Theatre surges with people yelling "VAVOOM!"

New church here.

There are lots of jokes from the emcees about the
Meso-American Long Count calendar's prediction of the end
of the world. On the twenty-first of December 2012, Earth will
collide with a black hole or with some random passing aster-
oid, perhaps even with another planet—kaboom—the end of
a 5,125-year cycle.

Or the start of a new era.

She thinks "post-apocalyptic" utopian, the great excitement—
call it desire—to have it all end so that we can make it anew,
better than before because now elemental, a world reduced to
what matters, creatural survival. And you *have* survived if you're
reading some piece of speculative fiction, or viewing a movie
made of it, or playing at "post" within a video game—that's
part of the utopian delusion, that you'd survive this re-making
of the calendar, the clock, the world . . .

—

OUT

That's a little of what she knows now: you don't survive—

At midnight, and home, she will look up "chupacabra" and learn another word, "cryptid," in Greek *krypto*, a creature or plant rumored to exist but whose reality is unrecognized by scientific consensus, the Yeti or the Loch Ness Monster, a Chupacabra, *chupar*: to suck, and *cabra*: goat, and so literally goat sucker, believed to suck the blood clean from domesticated livestock, particularly goats.

She has been out among the mythical. Chupacabra in his white spines, Li'l Chicken hung like a horse! Hung like two horses! How many goodly creatures are there here! My, my, my, How many? She is laughing . . . her bed piled with books.

. . . and she herself is now a Cougar, her graduate students tease her, even a television program by that name, hot middle-aged women on the make, and she marvels that widowed she is now made into a sexual predator, and indeed, men now hurry to inject "my wife" into an exchange of niceties, and if she is talking to a man at a party, particularly if they are laughing, the conversation lively, the wife is there by his side quickly, staking her claim. It makes her marvel, and she leaves having just arrived, dressed up and quiet and now even more quiet. Cougar. It meant "false deer," because of a cougar's unspotted coat. She had looked that up, too. Long ago. She pulled her long supple cougar tail around her like a stole, a garment the

83

past tense of "steal," but it was she herself she took off stealthily, the undulate golden fur of solitude wrapped around her. Cougars rarely, if ever, attacked humans—

"We can delight in the mythical," a friend tells her, "because we can control it." "No," another friend writes her, "no, we *are* the mythical."

—and that evening as she surges with others from beneath the temple ceiling held up by Aztec warriors, as she moves through the Hall of Feathered Serpents and pours forth onto the sidewalk in front of the Mayan Theatre, there is a cart set up in the gutter just beyond, and people gathered about, digging into their pockets for money, and then dispersing, holding paper plates up close to their faces as they feed the rolled tortillas into their poised mouths. "Street food, man! Completely fucking delicious!"

Could she find him, this satyr of the earlier evening? Could she drive slowly back down Pico Boulevard, her eyes dragging the sidewalks to find him still standing there with his great prong in silhouette against the gloaming sky? Could she give him money, feed him, make him focus on her face long enough to see her, as she had seen him, for that one brief instance, set off against the sky? A black man, his arms raised in triumph, greeting, exuberance; his arms raised in defeat, defiance, resistance. What had she seen, she asked herself, what?

—

She is supposed to want something, to have an appetite for something, for someone, she is not supposed to be a closed system, she knows this, says this to herself, *You are too encompassed, your life too hermetic, airless, not even a dog to run circles around your feet, to trip you out of your sphere,* but she does not get the dog, though she looks at so many pit bull rescues through the crosshatch of metal crates. She looks online at a baby corgi, its breeder's hands holding him forward, and at an ad for miniature bull terriers, like tiny sturdy tables with inscrutable faces—she looks because sometimes people will say at the house, "Oh, not even a dog," it is so quiet. They mean when they say this that they feel the stasis, the stultified quiet, and tonight driving home in her car she will manage to acknowledge a little hunger, and she will see her kitchen and its tiled counters and the white plastic cavern of the refrigerator lined with gelid offerings, and the fruit bowl in the breakfast room, clementines, a Pink Lady apple, the plastic lizard she lets live there—

Could she take a Myers-Briggs personality test on a dating website, this "type indicator" considered unethical to administer involuntarily, and so could she sit herself down and within the sophomoric publicity of the Internet voluntarily work out the type she was from the four dichotomies? Was she an extrovert or an introvert? She had been out and now she was in, and though she was pretty sure the sun would rise tomorrow, and in the many days to follow, she could intuit a different physics to the world altogether, and did she wear a mustache, oh not

—

often, but when she did only with pearls and amethysts. Could she answer the ninety-three "forced choice" questions in the Myers-Briggs personality test? How she loved the oxymoron of "forced choice," as she loved the oxymoron of "online presence," but there she was being quarrelsome again. Nanny goat.

She had tried once, but he accused her of not cleaning out a closet for him; he had said there was no room for him in her life. He couldn't see how slow and careful a person she was and this comment was like sand thrown in her face on the playground, puerile and petulant. How well she had been doing moving the furniture around in her heart, making a new front room. But now it had been five years since anyone had touched her, five years since she'd let the bone structure liquefy and the musculature surmount, but hers had been just another female body to him, he'd done this a thousand times, what he was supposed to do with a female body. It was called "having sex." She didn't think at her age she could become a woman who faked it, that mythical sex goddess who mothered a man into adequacy; it wasn't worth it to her to lie about such hope.

That was the problem, too, she could not get out of herself enough to accommodate the needs of someone else, the mind-fuck extremity was that it put one irretrievably at the center of an irretrievable self.

She knew from some lecture long ago that the word "tragedy" meant "goat song," though why was in contention. Was it because in Peloponnesian satyr plays the satyrs were goat-like rather than horselike? Maybe a goat was ritually sacrificed at some point during a play cycle and a Greek chorus sang as the knife came across the mohair throat, or maybe not that, maybe some mournful sound the goat made as it died, goat song, tragedy?

The front door of the gallery stood open, and she stood just apart from the people gathered in the twilight on the sidewalk, talking, small clear plastic cups in their hands. Curiously she noted that they all had their backs to the paintings in the windows. The paintings might have the exact time of completion painted on their canvases but no one seemed in a hurry to view them. She looked out across Ocean Avenue and through the trees of the park to the deep roar of the ocean in the distance. Inky light streaked the broad surface of the sea and the vast sky above as though one were being lifted from the other, the print from the printing block. Being cold had made her afraid, she knew, and so she'd walked quickly from the alley, challenging herself into warmth, her pistons sealed and tight and pumping her heart in her brisk walk. Now she looked through the open door and into the many people standing within the gallery, and finally to the woman with her liquid black hair.

The woman stood inside the gallery talking to a man in a black jacket over a black tee shirt. She watched the woman run her finger down to a point on a piece of paper, and then show it to him. He nodded, and the woman smiled and walked to a large canvas on the back wall and affixed a red dot beside the card. The woman passed for a moment into the back room and then emerged just as quickly, carrying bottles of wine in her arms. She settled the bottles on the table with the flowers and cups and then a man had his hand at her back and the woman stepped off with him, her head leaned down, listening to something he was saying.

The woman was so tall, and she watched her hem move about her legs as the woman walked, the hem she had sewn, and she watched the woman move in the gallery, and be nodded at and kissed on her cheeks, and she continued to watch the woman as she affixed another red circle beside a card, continued to watch as she entered the gallery and then she stood at the table, letting her backpack drop down her leg to puddle at a table leg. She organized the cups and the small napkins and cleaned off the table, the wine spills and the various screw tops. She lined up the tall green bottles of water from Italy. "Bottled at the source!" she read. She stationed the bottles of red wine in one place and the bottles of white wine in another and she thought of burning in hell for eternity, her fingers having now touched bottles containing alcohol. She hadn't drunk anything though, she defended herself, but to who, she quickly thought? Who was she now defending herself against?

"A glass of white wine," a young black man commanded, smiling, and she poured the cup full, and he said, "Whoa little pony. You only pour to about here," and he moved his index finger across the clear plastic about halfway down, or halfway up! she thought. She watched him take the full cup from her hand and reach for a paper napkin to hold beneath it, the man sipping off the top before he moved away. When she poured a cup of red wine for another man, she poured it just past half full and then passed it to him this time atop a napkin, both held out to him. That was simple enough wisdom, she could see, a napkin to catch spills, particularly red wine, she assumed, red wine that might stain, but she liked this elegant conveyance, too, a cup atop a napkin, even if the cup was only half full. Then she poured water for a mother and her son, and he smiled up at her sheepishly as he took the cup of spritzing water from her, the napkin beneath it something new to him, something he seemed to need to navigate, to stabilize the cup within. His eyes were riveted now as he drank and then his nose crinkled at the lively carbonation.

"Any lime?" the mother asked and she admitted that she didn't know, but she'd find out, and then she asked the mother, "So, you put a slice of lime in the water? That's how you serve it?" and the mother said, "Sure, if you have it, it's nice, a little flavor," and then the mother turned her back to her and moved her son along with her guiding hand at his back.

"You," the woman said, and that was all, *you*. "There's ice in the freezer and the tub for it is under my desk."

"Are there limes," she asked the woman, "for the water? Someone asked for limes?"

"Fuck me," the woman murmured, "what do they think this is, a bar?"

PARKING

"Of course," she'd meet her, "of course, at one, at Cucumber," and "yes," she knew where it was, the impossible parking situation, "yes," but their salads are delicious, Rosalind assured her, as though she did not know Cucumber and had never eaten there before, but she had, and had been struck by how rare a place Cucumber was in Los Angeles, fresh, straightforward food, muffins and cookies, salads, sandwiches, soups, "all made on the premises." Where she'd grown up, fresh, delicious, straightforward food was everywhere, and parking, too, and no one thought it even needed being said that food was made there, on the premises. A restaurant was *where* food was made—restaurant as middleman almost didn't exist.

She put the phone back in its stand and walked down the bright windowed hall of her apartment to her bedroom and reached her wallet out of her straw bag. Rosalind never paid, or even offered, and wasn't that so often the case, those rolling in it didn't spread it around for others to roll, even for a wee luncheon. She had a twenty-dollar bill and two ones, and if there was a parking meter to be placated, she'd get at most half of an hour with her four quarters now that the city was unapologetically predatory. "The city's so broke" everyone said, as though it was just fine to calibrate the meters so stingily, to generate civic funds by making tickets inevitable, and then wildly expensively out of whack with the nature of the infraction: twenty-five cents

—

91

past time filched seventy dollars out of your pocket—and any civic goodwill you might have ever harbored. Of course now what the city really wanted was you feeding a credit card into one of their new fangled meters with the lights and buttons and keypads. She wouldn't be doing that, she said to herself, parking on credit. Who carried a zero balance on their card, and what with compounding interest, who knew how much you'd end up paying for that hour's parking, what would be next! But the first time she'd been to Cucumber she'd driven the neighborhoods just north of Santa Monica Boulevard, trolling the residential streets for unrestricted parking, and there was none, not without a residential parking permit, not even for an hour or two. There was meandering block after meandering block of tidy Southern California homes with their sprinklered lawns sparkling in the sunlight, and the streets almost empty of cars.

Didn't she have a stash of quarters in a party favor toy purse beneath her vanity? Last time she'd had to relent and find a meter, and even then it was two blocks away and she'd had to leave the lunch table twice to feed the meter, but indeed, in the little plastic purse were eight quarters and she put them in her wallet with the other coins. She hoped she had quarters enough for an hour and a half.

In Rosalind's voice she'd heard what somehow she'd been expecting to hear for years now, the quality of outrage and terror that conveyed a husband's wandering. Rosalind had only asked if she could make it on such short notice, but of course she could, hearing what was in Rosalind's voice, and now she faced her open closet, fingering through the shirts, none of which she wanted to put on, let alone wear for the few hours she would be out of the house. God, what was she doing. She wasn't exactly bathed, but she wasn't exactly unbathed, either. She rubbed her hands up her forearms to see if she were sticky or not. She had made white and purple lisianthus blossoms all morning for a shower cake, a starlet having her first baby, and Georg, the baker, wanted forty-five more blossoms in a lighter shade of violet, and then stems and leaves, too. How big a baby shower was it? she wondered, shaking her head, but answers to questions like this were rarely forthcoming, and she made hundreds of sugar flowers for cakes she never saw for people whose names she would never know. "Filthy rich," was all Georg ever said. "Filthy rich," in his Swedish accent, and she figured he charged his customers thirty to forty times what he paid her to make his sugar flowers—the flowers he was famous for.

"Have you ever made lisianthus," he asked her two weeks ago.

"No," she said, "but I can. It's not a problem . . ." and already, in her mind's eye, she was rendering them in her folio, drawing the long straight stems, the sessile leaves, genus *Eustoma russellianum*.

"Customers who want exotic flowers—that's all I need," he growled.

"They're at every farmers' market, Georg. They're not exotic. They're also called prairie gentian, almost a wildflower. Christ almighty."

"Fine," he said. "They're not exotic."

"No, they're not exotic."

———

93

She stayed off the phone until he called back with the colors, a push-pull they did to each other, he not giving her all the details she needed so that she would then have to call him back, as though she worked for him, took her orders from him, when in fact, his cakes were bought in large part because of her work. She tried never to call him, unless the time was closing in. She didn't work fast, couldn't work fast, and he usually got nervous before she did. Often he wanted to see what she'd done so that he could pattern a cake's buttercream in trellis or basketweave or dotted Swiss. Recently he'd taken to pressing fondant against bamboo sushi mats to make the texture of a straw hat. She liked her clematis trailing against this fondant.

In twenty minutes the phone had sounded and he asked without preamble, "Purple—they grow in purple, right? And white?"

Georg! How nice of you to call back, she said in her head, tucking the phone into her shoulder, wiping her hands with a white towel. She kept her counsel for a moment longer, and then she said aloud, "varying shades of purple, and pink and white. Yes."

"It's a baby shower. I said that, right?"

"You said that." The kitchen had darkened in that way that afternoons occasionally, suddenly, lost their light. She could barely see the hellebore petals she'd been smoothing from sugar paste. She looked out at the street lined in cars and it seemed preternaturally still. Perhaps the way a cake is still, she thought, and then knew that to be an odd thought, or perhaps only a thought she might have, or Georg, or bakers looking up

—

94

from their careful work, something suddenly as still in the day as their trays and racks, their loaves of bread, their cakes.

"Three hundred and fifty dollars," Georg said, as though all she needed now was for him to get off the phone—and he'd oblige happily.

"No, no, no, Georg, that's not the way we're going to do this," she said.

"All this counting," he said dismissively. "It wears me out."

Do they hear themselves, she thought. Why was it all right for her to have to count, but not him?

"How many?" she had asked. "Let's start there. How many white and how many purple?"

Now she pulled a white linen shirt from a hanger, knowing she'd have to fight Georg over the added lisianthus, the forty-five violet ones he'd asked for this morning. They'd agreed on a price for fifty white blossoms and fifty purple, and there had been no mention of greenery in that first go-around. He needed her more than she needed him and yet it seemed she was always on edge, always worrying the tension over being paid, particularly when an order got added to. She could expose Georg, and he knew this, and she was becoming more willing to threaten exposure, not that she ever would—after all she had to live with herself and with her actions—but certainly she had become more willing to make it obvious to him that she could embarrass him hugely, and because of this, Georg got meaner and meaner. She didn't want to be mean back, wasn't constitutionally a mean person—she had studied to be a botanist, for Christ's sake—but his meanness was wearing on her and she felt willing to tighten the screws after

—

the Grossinger cake. *In Style* had reported the cake as costing ten thousand dollars; Georg had whined and complained and the check for six hundred dollars had not come until she threatened to hold back the sugar fairies she'd made for a child's birthday, delphiniums and fuchsias she'd put tiny faces within—all these sweet, celebratory creations—if people only knew the nastiness behind them.

She turned down Century Park East and drove through the deep corridor of mirrored office buildings and made the light turning left onto Santa Monica Boulevard. She began looking for a parking place, lamented that the San Francisco trick of looking for exhaust fumes blooming in the dense fog rarely worked in Los Angeles, and now in L.A., people sat in their cars, talking on cell phones, paying no attention to anyone trying to park. In San Francisco, people would kill you for that kind of inattention, that kind of rudeness, but L.A. thrived on rudeness, made it a virtue of one's presentation. The ruder someone was, then obviously the more important you were, and the more important you were, the more you would pay for a cake . . . and the more you would pay, obviously then the more important you were, and the more exalted the cake. Georg's cakes were delicious cakes, but they were two-hundred-dollar cakes at best without her work. What an asshole. She doubted he could even make a spun sugar nest for a croquembouche, though the thought of all of that hot caramel burning his hands made her smile. Then it appalled her how mean he was making her; how mean she was letting him make her, all this counting, all this fighting in order to make a living wage.

She spotted Cucumber up the small street, the old single-story brick building, but she didn't turn, thinking her chances for parking better farther down Santa Monica Boulevard. At a stoplight she looked up at a huge fuchsia-pink billboard.

1-877-MISS-JUNK

"WHEN YOUR JUNK WON'T FIT IN YOUR TRUNK—

WE'LL HAUL IT AWAY."

Miss Junk was a cartooned Playboy Bunny without the ears, but with a shelf of cleavage and long blonde hair. Miss Junk held something up in her black opera-length gloves that didn't exactly look like a huge full condom, but still, almost. This had to be a front for a prostitution ring. Junk! Come on! When your junk won't fit in your trunk! But maybe not.

She saw red brake lights and sped up through the green light, pushed on her blinkers, then just as suddenly put on her brakes and withstood the blaring of horns behind her. She waited for the driver to fasten his seatbelt, find his sunglasses, look at his iPhone, glance once out his side window at her wait-ing, press a few buttons on his phone's keypad and then gaze at himself in the rearview mirror. He looked down into his lap and started to speak and finally she relented and drove on.

Rosalind stood just inside the old glass door of Cucumber, her weight back on one leg, and the other leg thrust forward, and at its extremity, the beautiful expensive sandal against the mottled commercial linoleum. "I know!" Rosalind said. "Parking!"

"Not so much that even, just people not moving, people just sitting in their cars, yacking away on cell phones. I just have twenty minutes on my meter."

Rosalind's face didn't seem to register this last comment, but Rosalind's face looked calm to her, calmer than her voice had sounded on the telephone, but not placid, she thought to herself, and then she realized maybe Rosalind's face was a bit immobile, subdued, in shock perhaps, though she was covering this, acting within the moment what the moment necessitated, no more, no less.

"You still don't have a cell phone?" Rosalind asked, leaning down to kiss her, and it was one of those questions she was trying to learn to just let go by, to not argue with or reflect back. After all, years ago, when she'd lived in France for a semester, the smoking in the cafés had bothered her—she couldn't breathe—and someone told her to start smoking, that she'd be able to breathe and she'd known that this was just absurd enough to be correct, and it had been—the only time in her life that she'd smoked, and now she couldn't smoke even if she wanted to because it would give the mediums she worked in an odor. But she couldn't really afford a cell phone, or rather, of all the things she needed to afford, she didn't choose a cell phone as one of them. And sure, if she owned one, or if her business depended on them, cell phones wouldn't annoy her so much—that was no doubt true. But she couldn't hold a cellphone under her chin and talk on it, like she could her land line if she had to, and sure she could wire herself up like she was wearing a colostomy bag, the iPhone tucked into the pocket of her jeans, earbuds, but her concentration was off when she worked while on the phone, and the flowers seemed just good enough, no better. Instead of her usual botanical exactitude, that personal challenge to herself and to her first love, botany . . . instead the sugar flowers looked like foppish renderings rather than examinations or precise studies. She hated the difference in the work, just good enough as opposed to something that captured, say, the gradations of color of the anther at the end of a stamen. *Get the gonads right!* she'd say to herself, amused. *Gads, at least do that!*

"Someday I'll get one," she said now, simply, just letting Rosalind think her antique, reactionary, a Luddite, which in the truest sense of the term she was. She'd attended university in the midst of the turnover; one day there were dozens of work-study jobs, student librarians checking out books for people, and student traffic directors on the campus streets in white gloves, grooving their modernist dances as they facilitated cars going this way and that, amusing people while they waited, and the next day there were traffic lights and scanning machines, and people waiting dumbly, their faces inanimate, no one talking, no one delighting in youthful bodies moving ingeniously, usefully. Students had needed jobs, a little help getting them through; now they had more loans, and techno-gadgetry, and necessarily cars because they couldn't work on campus any longer—yes, she was a Luddite, people should have work, not machines, but she was pissing into the wind, as the expression went.

—

People's faces had been so alight watching the students direct traffic, people's eyes following the white-gloved hands moving willfully, up and down and across and then folded stiffly as though making animal beaks, and the arms straight as poles, the terrific dance, and in the library, the questions, "Paleobotany, wow, what's that?" or "Two weeks—can you get through something with 'biochemistry' in the title in two weeks?" No longer those exchanges, but rather a large scanning table with a huge light and a line of people angrily, silently waiting.

She'd dropped out at the beginning of her second year of graduate school when her loans reached fifty thousand, that number just staggering to her, and no calm that a job as a botanist would allow her to pay those loans off ever, let alone within twenty years. She hadn't gone to school to be in servitude to loans; she'd gone to school to be in service to a discipline and a profession perhaps, but not this, this yoke no matter how hard she had worked. As the loans mounted, so did her anxiety until she could think of almost nothing else, her mind a ticking meter, *how much is this costing me, this graduate student housing, this lecture, this lab, this bad food in the student center?* One day she'd sat down with a calculator and divided $50,000.00 by two years' worth of days. If she were just to pay back for 730 days, she would need $68.50 a day, and that's not even with interest. She wasn't contemporary, wasn't comfortable being leveraged up to her gills, and she knew she wasn't supposed to be so pointedly conscious of the debt, to calculate like this; she understood that she wasn't to know as profoundly as she did that she was being urged forward, lauded for striving—for becoming educated—and scolded at the same time, enabled and at once hobbled. It seemed she had one young lively leg leaping forward, and the other dragged along a heavy metal trap clamped to her foot.

"A cell phone. Yeah. Someday," she said again, knowing that expression wasn't even current, that it was now "smart phone" or "iPhone" or a . . . and she refused the name of a berry for a geegaw, a gadget. A keypad, no matter how tiny, could not ever be the deep purple-black aggregate drupes of a blackberry. Ever. She refused that replacement for Rosaceae Marion or Rosaceae Himalaya.

"Thank you," Rosalind said, moving with her index finger the shiny chestnut hair from her right eye. "I appreciate this. I'm sorry for the short notice."

They queued and gazed up at the menu chalked across several large panels of blackboard. She thought Rosalind looked calm, well turned out, or at least fashionably so, though perhaps more evidence of expenditure than style, the jeans trendy, costly, and too tight on her, the deconstructed shirts, one atop the other, their hems not hems, but frayed meanderings more odd than interesting. You're jealous, she said to herself, you'd like that clothing, even just one of those shirts. Instead, she grabbed armloads of men's white shirts from the thrift store, ten for ten dollars on certain days, and she cut off the cuffs so the sleeves came to her wrist and protected her forearms. She had been deconstructing shirts ever since she'd started working with sugar!

"You won't believe what's going on," Rosalind said, her

voice unguarded and now suddenly anxious. "Will you come to a party on Saturday—I mean, I need you to come to a party on Saturday, and watch. Can you?"

She was aware that it was not heretofore a party to which she had been invited, but now that Rosalind somehow and in some way needed her there, she would be coming . . . though still it wasn't exactly an invitation.

"Yes," she said simply, "I can come," but why she would be attending and for what purpose, she had no idea. To watch what or whom? In her mind she saw the beautiful poplar-surrounded yard up Coldwater Canyon and the cottage some distance from the house, at the bottom of what would most accurately be called "the park," and the amorphous dark pool made to look like a small lake with an island at its center. "I ordered the three-salad plate here last time," she commented. "They were good, especially the roasted fennel with sun-dried tomatoes."

"I'm not really that hungry," Rosalind said. "I just didn't know where else to meet you."

She knew that someone listening in would think her difficult if she said anything right now, if she said *Why didn't you just ask to come to my apartment? Why, if you weren't hungry, or didn't intend to eat lunch, would you make me get in a car and drive out and pay for a lunch that I already have in my refrigerator?* but she would be the unseemly one if she said anything, and this was not about her—it was Rosalind having the troubles.

—

"Are you eating then?" she asked, "because I'm happy with just a cappuccino if you're not."

"You know it's going to happen," Rosalind said, her angular face severe and beautiful, "and you assume it's going to happen, but still, when it does, it's like a bomb going off in your heart."

She didn't want to say *It's Phillip* or *Phillip's having an affair*, she didn't want to say what she thought it was before Rosalind said it definitively, even at the risk of seeming dim-witted, slow on the uptake. If she said anything, it would be as good as saying she knew something about Phillip's activities of late—and she knew nothing at all, merely the man she had observed in the past, what he seemed capable of, the dark hair allowed to fall just below the shoulders, his finger moving across the tiny screen of his iPhone, brisk and sensuous. He'd taken them to dinner, a chance to meet Rosalind's new friend, a sushi place up at the top of La Cienega with a view of Los Angeles, and she accepted the invitation, not ever getting much of a chance to eat sushi, and sure, he'd had the iPhone out even as he met her, it changing hands so that he could shake hers, and then as they sat at table his hand moving across the iPhone, within it, his hand seemingly leading to what he really wanted, to where he really wanted to be—she'd thought all those things but not deeply, not to the exclusion of Phillip as a nice guy, Phillip as Rosalind's busy husband, handsome Phillip, rich Phillip, the man who was paying for her dinner and whom she would see in true Los Angeles fashion once every two years, his wife's little asexual mouse of a friend, the stitch they occasionally thought to pick up and knit into an evening . . . and then let go.

—

"Cappuccinos," she posed to Rosalind now, in Cucumber. "We don't have to eat." The huge platters of artichokes and hazelnuts, of corn and black beans, of beets tossed in tarragon and orange zests—she looked down at this good food, at the celery root salad, the roasted asparagus. She had made a bowl of tuna salad and it was in the refrigerator at home; she would be all right, she said to herself, she could eat later. She'd chopped celery and red onion and pickles into the tuna, parsley, it was a good tuna salad.

"You can just come to the front of the line," the girl behind the counter said. "Two cappuccinos? Right?"

"Eat lunch," Rosalind said to her, "I'm paying," but she held her hand up to the girl, an affirmation, and moved them both to the cash register. "She's coming to the party on Saturday—I know it's her."

She wanted to remind Rosalind that that's why she'd married Phillip, that she'd liked his independence, his doing what he wanted to do, his not worrying social conventions, banal etiquette, money the unassailable license—all the attributes of his that had been so tremendously attractive to Rosalind, Phillip the mover and shaker, her ticket to ride, even if he left Rosalind flatlined in bed. She hadn't known Rosalind and Phillip ten years ago during their courtship, but Rosalind had related those early days to her shortly after they'd met, a chance meeting in a museum line, both of them alone, Courbet landscapes, then the lecture, which was excellent and funny, the older woman speaker characterizing herself as more of a barker for this artist than a docent, their laughter, the glances of shared mirth, the suggestion of a coffee together, sure, I have time, I'd like that. "So, what do you do," Rosalind had asked her.

"What do I do? Oh, landscapes, rather like Gustave Courbet," she answered, laughing, thinking of the cake she'd designed for the eightieth birthday of a famous geologist, and she'd drawn a picture for Rosalind of how the cake had to look for Georg, the various cutaway layers, a plateau formation, "layercake geology," and then she'd made a fallen cottonwood, golden columbines, purple fleabane, tiny sugar yucca plants to place beside a Virgin River made muddy with caramel. But she didn't describe any of that flora to Rosalind, couldn't really and keep Georg's fame intact—she'd signed a nondisclosure contract with noncompete clauses—and it hadn't mattered anyway because Rosalind poured out her life to her for almost an hour, she the complete stranger needed for such an enterprise. A complete stranger who knew how to listen and better yet, who barely knew any of the names Rosalind dropped or the parties Rosalind attended or the roles she'd narrowly missed out on and that now she did not pursue at all, her life elegantly in service to Phillip, his many needs, his home, the entertaining he wanted done. Rosalind still thought she was a landscape architect and even if the contract with Georg had run down long ago and he'd never gotten around to the lawyers again, to putting those contracts back in place, she found residing in the shadows restful and soothing and sane, her true self, and the sugar flowers she created, their exacting realism, her reasons for their precision—all shrouded from oversight or discussion. This was good with her. She could talk Southern California

—

gardening and xeriscaping as easily as she could the chemical properties of sugar in various states, whatever.

But, and she admitted this to herself, she was also saddened sometimes by how little people asked her about herself. *You're not a conversationalist,* her mother had always said, *so just get people talking about themselves—you'll be fine, and they'll love you for it,* and so she did just that, and indeed the Rosalinds of the world sought her out, poured their lives out to her and hours could go by and there would barely be a question directed at her, and it was fine, really, really it was fine, and yet it made her sad now, too. She had never known her father, never much known if there had in fact been a father and not a turkey-baster insemination, and whatever her actual genesis, that had always been fine, whatever it was or wasn't, but then two years ago her mother had died, which left almost no one to ask her about herself and to wait to actually hear.

She worked in her folio, drawing her floral studies, regressing one flower, her mother's favorite, a Lenten rose, all the way from full bloom back and back and back as though into a mirror, bud and then seedling . . . all the way to its cells, its mitochondria with a mitochondria's independent genome, that singular inheritance from a mother, uniparental, as she seemed to be, she thought fancifully, a product of one, her mother's parthenogenic daughter.

Now she said to the girl perched on a high stool at the cash register, "Could you make my cappuccino with whole milk." They all wore black caps and black chef's jackets, even the ones taking the money.

—

"We use two-percent milk," the girl said, waiting on Rosalind's money.

"I think that's why she's making a request," Rosalind said sweetly.

"I don't think we have whole milk," the girl said.

"Your baking's done on premises, yes?" she asked, and the girl nodded enthusiastically. "Well, then you have whole milk."

Finally the girl left her high stool, and went to the cappuccino machine and conversed with a tall young man who said, "Yeah, no problem." He hunkered down and pulled from the undercounter fridge a gallon of milk, and she saw that it was whole and then moved off to find them a table along the front windows. She'd been watching over her shoulder as they stood in line, and now she pounced, a single man rising from his chair, wiping his face with a black paper napkin and then extracting his tie from where he'd tucked it between his shirt buttons. She slung her straw purse across the chair back and then gathered his dishes, the wreckage of a sandwich amid corn slaw, a dripping iced tea glass, but the busboy was there, taking them from her, swabbing the table with a wet towel, his face worried. "Gracias," she said, but his face said nothing back, his eyes cast downward. She supposed she should have just claimed the table with her purse and then gestured to catch the busboy's eye, but she didn't want to seem imperious, demanding. Maybe always it was a little unseemly to direct others, maybe? *But you're not superfluous*, she wanted to say to him, *I didn't mean to do your job*. Today it seemed that even a momentary lull in service, a missed duty, some minor slack picked up by a customer, could

—

give management the idea that a position wasn't needed, that a worker could be axed. She understood his anxiety, as though a dark contagion of efficiency experts hung over everyone, contracting people into joblessness. The busboy moved away from her and then he stooped to pick up the scrunched paper worm of a straw wrapper. He wadded it with one hand and then tossed the white paper pill expertly across a distance of floor into a bin of dirty dishes.

"How'd you know that?" Rosalind asked, bringing their cappuccinos to the table, the spoons rattling in the saucers. "About the milk?"

"Chemistry," she said.

Rosalind looked at her, puzzled. "What about it?"

She laughed a little. "Baking chemistry?" but then Rosalind's face fell into shadow—Rosalind thought she was laughing at her. But she wasn't. She pulled the heavy oak chair out and sat down. "Flour likes fat," she said. "Needs it to plump."

"I must be like flour then—" Rosalind said.

"Oh, come on, you're thin enough."

"Thin enough for what."

She rose quickly from the chair and fetched sugar packets, but then walking back to the table she realized there were large irregular brown sugar cubes sitting within the bowls of the spoons placed to the side of the cappuccinos. "Whoops," she said, "I didn't see those beautiful cubes."

"It's just a firm party," Rosalind said. "It's why I didn't invite you before—you'll be bored to tears. Investment bankers are unrelievedly boring!"

—

"I don't expect to be invited to all manner of events, okay? Please."

"But you'll come?" Rosalind asked. "I mean, why it matters I know who it is he's fucking this time, I don't know, but it does."

"This isn't the first time?" she asked.

"Of course it's not the first time—it's just usually I know who it is, and it's just a quick dip, nothing more, but something's different this time. I can feel it."

"I think I'm not understanding, because it seems like you do know who it is . . . and why hasn't it mattered before now?"

"It just hasn't. These girls, they're like party favors, swag, they let themselves get handed around. He came home, you know, whatever. He had a wife, and I was that wife, and he came home to me. For the most part he was there."

She let the brown cube drop through the pillowy milk foam, a boulder through cloud cover. "You think he's in love with this . . . one," she said, pausing on the word, wanting to use a real word, "woman" or "lover" or some word accurate to the situation. At heart she was a botanist; she admired classification, found it stabilizing.

"Phillip. In love? I don't think so. God, what the hell would *that* look like?"

"I'm sorry, Rosalind. I'm real slow sometimes, so you'll have to tell me what the problem seems to be." She thought she sounded like a minister, a middle-aged nurse, *What seems to be the problem?* But she thought she might know already, thought she might not even need to see with her eyes . . . the girl, the woman, the lover—*She's pregnant, Rosalind, pregnant with Phillip's child—that's the difference, and he may now be just old enough he's sentimental about it, changed his mind on babies, thinks it might be just fine to leave a few copies of himself behind.* She said instead, "You think he's going to abandon you over this one," and then looking at Rosalind's face, she realized she'd used a terrible word, that even the word "divorce" would have been better.

"Do you have to feed your meter?" Rosalind asked.

She didn't, she had seven more minutes. She tasted her cappuccino and it tasted good, fully fatted and sweet. Besides the added flowers she needed to make, she had to do about twenty lisianthus leaves, too, and stems, the blue-gray-green not exactly right yet, though almost, almost, but lunch hadn't cost her but a few quarters, she thought, and this was good because her drawing folios were almost two hundred dollars, and she now needed a new one. She had worked on lisianthus in the last pages, two days capturing the swirled purple and green of an unopened bud, and the interesting blue-gray leaves spaced far down the stem, the way the leaves emerged without an axil or separation, as though the stem grew up through the leaf. Finally she'd gotten the leaves right, and now she slid down a little in this hard chair, enjoying her coffee, flattered, really, that Rosalind had called her. She had five mintues and then she'd have to plug the meter . . . though actually she needed to go. She didn't want to be up all night working on the rest of Georg's order.

—

"Phillip likes you," Rosalind said, looking across at her seriously. She doubted Phillip could conjure her name if he had to, let alone pick her face out in a line-up. "He won't suspect that you're watching him. You always watch anyway," Rosalind added.

"Yes," she said, "I do. My bad habits. What time is the party?"

"Seven—her name's Lissy," Rosalind said.

"Really?"

"Yes. Why? Is that strange?"

"Elisabeth?" she asked. "With an *s*? Lissy?"

"I guess, yes, probably. I don't know. I didn't think about it."

She finished her cappuccino and set the cup down in its saucer, hitting the spoon that then rattled quietly. She reached into her straw bag and pulled out a small tablet of paper and her pen case. She drew a tall length of stem and then a tightly furled bud at its top and then a fuller bloom at its middle. She labeled it by its genus not its common name and then pushed it across the table at Rosalind. "*Eustoma russellianum*," she said. "It means 'beautiful mouth,' *eustoma* does. Like yours," she added. "Just something I've been working on."

"I didn't know you were that good," Rosalind murmured.

"No one knows I'm that good," she said, laughing, but Rosalind's face clouded up again. "I'm laughing at myself," she reassured her, "not you. I think you think I'm laughing at you."

"I know. It's just suddenly I realize I don't really know you that well, but I should. I mean, how many years is it, now? And that's a very good drawing."

—

"It's a lisianthus, sometimes called prairie gentian, but Lissy, the name." She didn't say, nor had she written it on the drawing, that "lisianthus," a Greek word, meant the "flower of dissolution." She didn't need to point up all of these coincidences, if indeed they were coincidences. Was inevitability really a coincidence? She didn't know, but she certainly didn't need to add the finer points of classification to Rosalind's situation. It was what it was, or it was going to be what it was going to be. Though what exactly this situation was was a question she had. Girls like party favors, she heard Rosalind saying, throwaways, but Rosalind had also known in her heart of hearts that someday, there'd be one who wasn't just swag, who wasn't just an expensive giveaway that accrued from doing business with rich men. Rosalind seemed to understand these transactions, what they did and did not mean, but Rosalind also, seemingly, had understood that one day one of these other women would displace her. Rosalind knew this, but had gone along, or seemed willing to go as far as it took her? But then, as Rosalind said, it had been like a bomb going off in her heart. So Rosalind knew this . . . and yet she hadn't or hadn't allowed that it would hurt like hell, that it would destroy something? *You won't believe what's going on*, Rosalind had said, and yet it all seemed a usual set of occurences, of facts. She felt relieved that she had a meter ticking, that she had to get out of there.

"That's what you studied, right, botany?" Rosalind was saying now, grabbing, it seemed, for details vague in her memory.

"Thank you," she said to Rosalind, "for the cappuccino. I really need to get home," and she put her pen back in its slim zippered case and tucked the tablet of paper into her straw bag. She started to slide out of her chair, but Rosalind reached across and grasped her wrist.

"Stay," Rosalind whispered, "just for a little while longer."

She looked out the window at the sound of the meter maid's cart. She'd have a ticket for sure if she didn't run now—maybe even if she did run. "See you Saturday," she said, pulling her wrist out from under Rosalind's cool fingers, her beautiful rings, their cool brilliant gems. I'll need a five-dollar bill for the valets at their house on Saturday, she thought to herself.

"Stay," Rosalind whispered again. "Please."

Already she felt angry at Rosalind's beautiful mouth imploring her. She would be furious seeing the white slip of a parking ticket tucked beneath her windshield wiper blade. It would cost her almost an entire day of making flowers just to pay this minor infraction, probably sixty or seventy dollars, but what kind of person would she be if she didn't sit back down and listen? When had she become a person who didn't help others? The straw handle of her purse felt rough beneath her fingertips. How would she live with herself when she got home? But worse, and she knew this peril as well as she knew anything about herself, or about the day, or about days amid days and herself within them practicing her saccharinated botany—she knew that any flowers she made today, finally back at home, in the slow fade of light, cutting out the petals and smoothing them, thinning them, working the petals into their crepey realism . . . she knew that none of them would be exactly right if she did not straighten herself back forward in the chair and lis-

—

ten. Well formed, the flowers, yes, but limply so, begrudgingly so, spiritless. There was such a thing as work, and one could be paid for it, but there were elements of production that could never be compelled by numbers or reason or even technique. She could and would make the rest of these lisianthuses today, the paste within her fingers reproducing one after another, over and over again, the intricate hypertrophy, and almost no one would notice the difference in the flowers if she made them unhappily, flowers forced into being by the hands of someone who could not take a few hours out of her day to listen to a friend. She would know and the flowers would know. It was the difference between hurried robotic reproduction and creation, blossoming, and Georg would know, and he would work with them anyway, clustering the flowers in such a way that individual perfection displayed itself less . . . but Georg did know, and would know if today's flowers were not right, and he would look at her sadly, thinking it was about money, about being paid, about their constant struggle. *I'm sorry*, he'd say, *I can't pay you much more. My overhead is outrageous*, and she knew this to be true, and she knew that his clientele were not really "his clientele," because they would change their baker in a heartbeat, have their assistants call to cancel a cake already baked, or not even cancel, just let Georg find out from wedding details published in the magazines, an interview with the bride or with the wedding planner, a baker in New York, the cake being flown in. It had happened more times than either of them cared to mention, though Georg was still known worldwide, still the only baker most anyone could actually name in

—

Los Angeles. And their cakes were still the most beautiful, Georg's and hers.

"Did you . . ." she began, letting the woven straw handle slip back down across the chair back, ". . . did you and Phillip ever want to have children? Forgive me for asking such a difficult and personal question. It's none of my business."

Rosalind looked at her and then looked down, and then looked up again. "We had a child."

"I didn't know."

"She lived for seven days. Maybe you want to draw that picture for me," Rosalind said. "Maybe tell me what fucking species she was."

The suddenness of Rosalind's anger nailed her to her chair. She felt the hardwood against the backs of her thighs, the edge of the wooden seat up against the tendons of her knees, felt this and also felt inert, incapable of moving, her vertebrae flush against the hard chair back, and then before she could say anything, before she could fathom what to say, Rosalind's voice sprang across the table at her, "That's it, isn't it. Phillip's gotten her pregnant and she's so fucking young it's healthy as an apple cart."

"I don't know," she said, faltering. "Maybe. Probably. I don't know," and now any anger she had had earlier about the parking ticket and money necessarily had to be set aside, subdued. This is expensive, she thought to herself, and she felt it in her chest, an ache across her breasts, but it was not about money. To be sure, money would always be costing its cost in the background, in the foreground, no matter what, but this other was

—

expense she was out of practice in knowing how to afford. She'd been good at this once, she reminded herself, she'd been good to her mother, good to others, talked to people, joked with the assistants at the university, saw her professors as creatural beings, not encyclopedic monoliths—she'd been a good person once and it hadn't been a calibration, a transaction, she hadn't thought twice about her time, about who she gave it to, about how she lived within it with others.

"I didn't want to burden anyone," Rosalind said. "I didn't want to burden you. I actually hardly know you."

"No," she said, desperation in her voice, "no, I want to hear. The baby, it—she—was teratogenic—"

Incredulity and acknowledgment gathered uncomfortably together in Rosalind's eyes, her face shattered and immobile at once. Rosalind stared at her across the table, a slow-motion explosion with almost no sound. "You and your fucking words, eustoma whatever, tera-whatever."

"It was nature," she said quietly, "and not your fault, not really even much your doing. These babies happen."

"Tell that to Phillip."

"He can't possibly blame you," she said.

"Know how he does," Rosalind said briskly, raising her eyebrows, her mouth stretched into a smirk. "I refused to abort her even when we knew there were possibly problems. I thought okay, she might have a withered limb, be a dwarf, whatever, but if her mind was there, what would it really matter, and they just didn't know, it was too early, and so I refused any more ultrasounds, any more inspection—I didn't want to have

—

to fight them all. I took her away—I thought I'll make this baby on my own—fuck them and all of their machinery."

Phillip loomed in her mind, his dark hair sweeping down against the pale blue shirt collar in the dim lighting of the restaurant, the huge bottle of Onikoroshi being poured by the waiter into small clear glasses set in dishes, the clear sake pouring out and then flowing up and over the tops of the glasses. She could see Phillip lift his glass, dripping with sake, and drink, the droplets down his shirtfront, devil-may-care. He was an embodiment of satiety and license and cool willfulness, and his handsomeness was such that one almost didn't want much else from him. "Rosalind," she began, "that's not really the kind of thing Phillip was ever going to be able to cope with, no matter how much money . . . no matter really even if he'd been willing to try. You knew him well enough to know that. You carried her to term. You made your decision a long time ago. I mean, about Phillip."

The meter maid's cart was no longer just out the window on the street, and the murmur and bustle of the restaurant continued, though it seemed to her quieter, its sound on mute, perhaps because people were listening to them. And then she realized people were listening, that there were no conversations at the tables on either side of them. People were watching them out of the corners of their eyes, their forks raised to their mouths.

"Who's in your life?" Rosalind asked. "Why are you such an authority—"

"I'm not."

—

"You and your mother—that's the relationship in your life—why should I listen to you?"

Yes, why? she thought. Why should anyone listen to a thing she said? And what if she told Rosalind in this awkward and angry moment that her mother had died two years ago, what if she exercised a small virtue, a kind of raw honest exchange, what would it matter? Rosalind's news shouldn't be trumped, or equaled or displaced, she knew this, and knowing this was another small virtue, but somehow virtues—no matter which ones she chose—barely mattered. "I don't know," she said, and her voice sounded too plaintive, or maybe just too sad, too exhausted. She wanted to know if there had been an early cranial measurement? She was sure there had been, but it had perhaps been normal, that was possible. She resorted to what she often resorted to, drawing some leaf or petal in her mind, a dogwood blossom on a black bough, a peony, naming its parts, but then she saw the little faces she'd made within the corolla of the fuchsias and the purple-blue delphiniums, the tiny fairy faces that at first she'd resisted making, the botanical fidelity of the flowers being her challenge and her accomplishment, but Georg had pushed and pushed and pushed until she'd consented. "The cake is for kids," he kept saying over the phone. "Children! Fantasy! The imagination! Remember?" he exhorted her. "Kids! You don't remember," and the disappointment in his voice seemed not for himself, not for his own mercantile struggles, but sadness for her. She had never been a child, he surmised. Never quite allowed to be.

"Leafy sea dragons," she said now across the table, not

really meaning to say this, and then she just went with it. "Have you ever seen them?" she asked Rosalind's puzzled, angry face. "They're sort of fantastical, half flora, half fauna—what I'm trying to say, and what you'll probably hate me for saying, is that I think I understand the decision you made, just to see how she'd come out, just to see what kind of child she might be? She didn't have to be anything you'd ever seen a child be. You were willing to just meet up with her however she came out."

The busboy reached down and picked up her empty cappuccino cup and the spoon tumbled out of the saucer onto the table spewing a pale brown comet across the drawing. Rosalind looked up sharply at the busboy, at his back as he sped away, and then she looked down at the paper and drew her finger gently across the coffee, trying to lift it from the paper.

"It's lunchtime," she said to Rosalind. She could feel the crush of people behind her, lined up out the door now, but she didn't turn to look. "They want our table."

Rosalind seemed to not hear her, or to ignore the urgency of the restaurant's needs around. "No," she finally said. "I don't think I was that . . . you're making me out to be far more conscious of the range of deformities than I was at the time. I was never that brave, or even that stupid. I thought dwarf or a midget, clubfeet, whatever, I don't know . . . but . . . and I know this *is* stupid, I never expected her not to be viable, not to be able to live. It didn't occur to me that she'd die anyway. To abort her would have been far more humane—for everyone. Don't you need to go, or to pay the meter?" Rosalind asked. "Or something. Don't you need to get home?"

—

But the pressure of the ticket had been removed, the ticking meter—let it tick, she thought—or somehow now it wasn't ticking and the restaurant continued to sound muted, as though its soundtrack had been turned down to just a few decibels. "I already have a ticket, I'm sure. It doesn't matter. I'm sorry that I let it seem like it mattered—obviously it's not important."

"It was a few minutes ago," Rosalind said. Her cappuccino sat before her untouched, its billow of foam residing. She held the drawing of the lisianthus, and she moved the index finger of her other hand up and down along its straight narrow stem, and then along the perpendicular streak of coffee now soaked through to the back. Rosalind turned her head slowly and looked out the front window of the restaurant. The sunlight cast down along her perfect cheeks, and her entire face so deeply drawn into itself seemed carved from alabaster.

"Rosalind," she said, looking at her keenly. "Would you have time to come to my apartment? Now? Today? I could show you what I'm working on, not because I need to get back—I mean, I do need to get back—but I'd like to show you what I make in the world. You don't know what I do because I've never really told you what I do, and I've never shown you and I've never invited you to see. It's not your inattention—you haven't been a bad friend! There are reasons other than a lack of hospitality on my part, too, but they're not good enough reasons I realize now—"

—and then she and Rosalind stood in her kitchen, Rosalind's fine sandals against the pristine but worn white linoleum and Rosalind's eyes alight, exclaiming, *my god*. Rosalind moved slowly, turning, gazing along the counters and into the glassed-in cupboards lined with sugar flowers. Even though the purse was small and elegant, she reached for it hanging from Rosalind's shoulder. "Let me take that," she said. "Just so we don't knock anything," and she took and placed both Rosalind's slim purse and her own straw bag on her kitchen stool by the door. "Hellebore," she said, going down the rows with Rosalind's gaze, "*Alchemilla mollis*, or lady's mantle. La Minuet—it's a small hybridized rose—those are just asters. Clematis, which I love making, and that's another kind of hellebore, a Lenten rose, my mother's favorite."

Rosalind pointed at the center crowns in the Lenten roses: "Stamens," she told her.

"That color," Rosalind said.

"I made them for my mother. She died. I know you don't know that, that I didn't tell you. 'When your junk won't fit in your trunk—we'll haul it away,'" she said. "I'm getting things off my chest, I guess."

"That's such a weird billboard, isn't it?"

"I think it's a front for something."

"Maybe. I'm sorry about your mother."

Rosalind continued around the kitchen and then her eyes gathered up the dining table covered in clear plastic egg bins, the lisianthus blossoms and buds resting or placed across the cups. There were stacks of clear plastic shoe boxes lined with rows upon rows of flowers standing up in Styrofoam. "That's how you transport them, yes?"

She nodded her head as she watched Rosalind trace with

—

121

her eyes the long, straight stems, the buds, the blooms, and then the two tea towels covered in leaves. "I couldn't get the color right," she told her. "They have this distinctive blue-gray-green color."

"You're a perfectionist."

She thought to herself, No, I'm a botanist, but she said aloud, "It doesn't really matter much."

"It matters to you."

"Yes, it matters to me."

"Georg's. Right? You're the one behind all those wildly expensive cakes?"

"It'd be best if you said nothing. He does in fact bake the cakes themselves. There used to be a contract, but it ran out."

"What do you mean a contract?" Rosalind asked.

"Very much like one a butler signs if he works for a very famous person, that he won't divulge anything about his employer, or the family, not even what their everyday china is, or their perfume, that sort of thing, and so I am not ever to divulge that I make all the sugar flowers."

"Really?" Rosalind said. "That seems a little overly proprietary. I mean, certainly a baker like that has an entire crew of assistants or baby bakers or whatever. Certainly they know."

"Still, it's my livelihood, my only income—and I made a promise. And some days it's okay with me that everyone thinks Georg makes these, and some days it's not. There are only a few people in the world who work at this level of detail, you know, and so it's probably right to protect the exclusivity. I don't know—it pays my rent."

—

"The contract is really about you selling only to him. You know that, don't you? That's what he's protecting, his source. It had a noncompete clause, yes?"

"I don't know," she said.

"You can't sell to anyone else, right?"

"No, I can't. I mean, I guess I could now but I don't. I wouldn't. It's not like there's a huge demand—or even a huge appreciation for it."

"Your mother, where is she—"

"You mean, Where did I bury her?" she asked, alarmed and instantly sad, hadn't Rosalind been listening to her?

"Yes. Where . . . where did you put her to rest? Silly expression—they're not napping in the next room."

"I didn't know what to do, where to put her, or whether to bury her or not. I didn't feel I had anyone I could ask."

"Nine million people, or thirteen million people, whatever the number is and I didn't know who to ask either. I didn't know what to do with a baby's ashes. Though there aren't a lot of ashes with a baby. I had gone away."

"But you knew to have her cremated?"

"I didn't know anything, other than I couldn't very well take a casket with me, or a gravesite."

"I couldn't actually afford to bury my mother anywhere. After a time, I realized that. So, she's here, with me. I have her ashes. They're just in a cardboard box."

Rosalind looked at her closely. "Really," Rosalind asked. "Just a cardboard box?"

She was still holding her car keys and the parking ticket. She

—

was always careful not to put anything in her kitchen other than food, her flowers, her work. It was inviolable space—inviolable space that was clean and potentiating. She had work to do, slow, careful work that did not go well if rushed. She felt stymied by Rosalind's question, Rosalind's obvious discomfort with human remains in cardboard. "I moved, " she said stupidly, as though this might explain. "After my mother died. This is smaller, and the rent's better."

"Ventura," Rosalind responded, but she hadn't asked Rosalind where she'd gone, where she'd been. "I found a little furnished apartment near the beach. It was very shabby—it all was shabby, and I was shabby, and I felt like I was in another era, or that's what I talked myself into, that I was like an unmarried pregnant woman a hundred years ago."

"Phillip sent you money?"

"He kept paying the credit cards, if that's what you mean."

"Did they have credit cards a hundred years ago?!" She laughed, and Rosalind's face gentled and smiled. "Did he come toward the end?" she asked.

"You don't know it's the end," Rosalind said. "You think it's the beginning."

"You know what I mean."

"Come anyway, on Saturday," Rosalind said. "Please."

"It's all very expensive, whether we want it to be or not. Isn't it?" But Rosalind didn't answer her. She continued speaking, she felt she needed to. "How do you feel about Phillip bringing someone into your own home, someone who might be pregnant with his child?"

"You've helped me figure it out. I think you're right," Rosalind said, and then she lifted her head, her hair tossing. "Your mother, she didn't leave you anything? Not even a house or something? Jewelry? Something you could liquidate?"

"No."

"You dropped out of school—out of graduate school?"

"Yes. Because of debt. It just seemed like such an inordinate burden, like I'd never be able to pay it off, and I haven't, even the debt I had, have—it won't be paid for several years. My mother could barely work, and finally I don't think my mother was actually equipped psychologically to attend to practical matters. She was sort of wise, though, or at least I used to think so. But maybe I scuttled my chances, too, because in taking care of her I was too careful of everything, too vigilant. You have to be able to be a little delusional to live, it seems to me, to be a little devil-may-care. You can't be aware of the ticking meter and I was, all of the time, even as a child. I used to bring home half of my school lunch to feed my mother in the evenings. If I could get us to the next day, we'd be okay. I'd bring home the roll and the cookie, the piece of fruit, and the extra carton of milk they'd happily give you if they thought you'd drink it. I was so polite, so deferential, didn't cause problems and so no one watched me, and I stole toilet paper from the bathrooms, one roll a week, until they started using the huge industrial rolls."

She could see in Rosalind's eyes that she'd said too much, gone too far, could see the look of embarrassment for her in Rosalind's eyes. *Keep them talking about themselves*, she heard her mother say. But the problem was also Los Angeles, and you didn't talk about being down and out in Los Angeles, it just wasn't what anyone wanted to hear, realism, in a town where projections were the main industry.

Rosalind stood by her table looking down at the several stacked bins. "The lisianthuses?" Rosalind asked. "What are they for?"

"A shower cake. A baby shower."

"You don't think—"

"No, I don't think. Lissy, lisianthus, a baby shower—it's a coincidence—it's for some starlet anyway."

"You don't think Phillip could be involved with a starlet?" Rosalind asked, some strange snobbery emerging. "You have work to do," Rosalind then said sadly. "I know I need to leave you to do it."

Rosalind took up her purse from the kitchen stool and placed the strap across her shoulder, and then turned to her and said, "That's what she is. Some young actress who had a role in a pilot that didn't lead to a series. So! in *that* case!" Rosalind exclaimed sarcastically, acting the airhead, dingbat young woman, "I'll just have a baby with someone else's husband! All will be well!"

The acid of the moment seared the air in the room, and she regretted for an instant inviting Rosalind into her apartment, this small inviolable space that she felt was the one province she had in the world, the one place that wasn't always ticking at her, though she knew, of course, it was too, the rent, the electricity, the water, she knew, yes, of course, she knew, but somehow, here, amid the work, she could for-

—

get that, or transform it into something greater, untouchable by those meters.

"Rosalind, I think you did the right thing for yourself, and for what you hoped would be your child," but she spoke this aloud to an empty kitchen, or not empty, she thought to herself. She could hear Rosalind starting her car in the street just beyond her windows. She turned on her oven to 150 degrees because she would need to make sure these flowers were hardened enough. She wiped down her small rolling pins, lengths of broom handle really, and a narrow test tube that had once held something in a lab so long ago she did not exactly remember. She gathered for a moment what she had to do, how much paste she had made, how much of the pale violet she'd colored, how much of the deeper purple, whether she needed more. And then the yellow-green of the buds that wasn't the gray-green of the leaves. She didn't usually work at the table, or work sitting down, but now she pulled the single chair out. If it was true that these were for a shower cake for the woman carrying Phillip's baby, she didn't exactly know what that changed for her, if it actually did change anything for her. What did Rosalind expect, she thought to herself, and then felt chagrined for thinking it. "We all make contracts," she whispered, and she could feel her breath across her hands. They protect one thing and lock us out of something else. It wasn't rocket science— knowing this, or really any kind of science, and yet we thought it was, regarded it as such, cause and effect, good behavior leading to good result, forgiveness that would then ensure fidelity. How we wished.

—

She rolled small swatches of the paste and then cut petals and thinned their edges with her thumbs or with a large marble that would occasionally roll from the table and that she'd have to hunker down on the floor and hunt up. This didn't happen when she stood at the counter and worked, the counter that had a tile lip against which the marble rested. If Rosalind knew about Phillip's many trysts, or if she looked the other way, certainly she'd have to know that one day it would be different, and Rosalind did know that—she'd said so herself—and now it was different, and there was someone else. Or there was a baby, and that trumped them all, a baby.

As the light came down into the day, deepening, she furled the petals around toothpicks to render them supple, organic-looking. It would probably be a very beautiful, perfect baby. She wanted to encourage that possibility with lisianthuses that looked as though they'd pushed up through soil to come into bloom in the sunlight of a wild prairie.

She didn't much romanticize babies, think them innocent, faultless beings. A baby, left to its own devices inside a woman's body, would take positively every bit of nutrient and calcium it needed, regardless. Even the babies that weren't going to be babies in the world did this. Still, she painted the petals with water, pressing them together, bloom after bloom emerging, and by twilight her arms resting on the tabletop were surrounded by purple lisianthuses.

"They don't taste good, right?" Rosalind had asked just before leaving.

No, she thought to herself now, they merely taste sweet, like

—

wishful thinking, like hope, just sugar and glycerine and glu-
cose and gelatin. She realized she had a punishing headache,
her temples like two doors coming closed against her head, and
she startled, realizing she hadn't made anything for her mother
to eat, not even soup and crackers, and she sucked in her breath,
mortified, and then she remembered.

She was no one's daughter any longer, and she was no one's
mother, either, and what she now owed in the world that way
wasn't very costly. She didn't have to be there for anyone, really.
She had some friends who called her occasionally, and she'd
answer to their needs as best she could, though today she had
perhaps not done well with Rosalind, but she'd gone, and she'd
found out things that she didn't know, about a life she hadn't
known had existed, even if just for a few months. Perhaps there
was this coincidence with the cake, or there was indeed this
coincidence, the request for lisianthuses because the shower was
for someone named or nicknamed Lissy. And Lissy seemed to
be pregnant by her friend's husband, and now her friend might
be becoming single again, might be being pushed from her
home . . . and some moments that seemed inordinately sad,
harrowing really, as she formed a tightly furled bud, or a leaf,
and some moments, it just seemed like inevitability, like So
what? she thought, holding a full-blown flower out before her
to inspect. In those moments she had a hard time knowing why
any of this mattered.

She had to let go of the fact that a good portion of today's
work would be in order to pay a parking ticket, expense laid
over expense. She missed her mother. *Just get them talking*

—

about themselves, she could hear her mother instructing her again, and they would, they would all go on talking about themselves, but that was good, and she knew that was good, and her mother would have been philosophical about the parking ticket, *the cost of doing business*, her mother might have said, *the cost of being here.*

SHE

Not knowing where to put the trash, the used paper napkins, the bottle caps, the screwtops from the wine, she'd unzipped the empty front pouch of her backpack and had been loading it up, but when she realized that used plastic cups needed more space than that to be disposed of, she ventured to gaze about for a bin for trash, and then to walk back to the office again, where she'd gotten ice and the tub for ice. The gallery, and the office, both were sleek and white and bright and clean, and she loved them immediately now in this suspended minute of allowing herself to gaze. The woman was quickly behind her, her face alarmed, ready to proclaim, but she said to the woman calmly, "I was just looking for something for trash—I've been putting stuff in my backpack—trash, I mean—but now there are cups and bottles."

"Oh," the woman said, a breath of surprise and relief, "yes, of course," and then the woman said, "I'm sorry. I know you've been really helping me tonight. I don't know where the fuck that bartender was, but there are all sorts of street people in Santa Monica, and no, you don't exactly seem like a street person, I mean, you're obviously not, or maybe you are, I don't know. You're a tad confusing, let me assure you—" and the woman continued talking but she was no longer hearing her words precisely, the woman's perfect coral lipstick moving on her lips, her dark eyes intelligent, her black hair moving in its sheets, its wings, sliding this way and that. She heard two words, two words the woman had already spoken, and then these two words she spoke again, *I'm sorry*, as the woman handed her a shopping bag with handles, "I'm sorry. This will have to do for now, okay. Just put it under the table. We'll get something tomorrow."

Close to nine o'clock on her grandmother's small watch, the gallery emptied, not in a rush, they weren't racing out, and yet it was almost immediate, the room full of people and talking and music, and then a few footfalls, the snap of a plastic cup set down, a word called out, "Lunch!" and then just the music, a guitar, she guessed, and perhaps drums. She had heard so little musical instrumentation in her life, she wasn't sure. In the New Testament there were no musical instruments mentioned, and God did not make mistakes, and thus the only music she had ever really heard and listened to was a cappella singing in church, and "a cappella" meant "as in a chapel," and so her father said that even though it was a papist word, it reflected the true sentiments of God and what God wanted, only the high and faltering and fluttering voices of his true believers.

Once she'd seen a man playing a small concertina, no bigger than a five-pound bag of sugar. He sat on an up-ended orange crate on the sidewalk in Needles, and she watched, fascinated, as his hands moved the bellows in and out, his fingers working the buttons. He smiled at her and teeth were missing here and there and he had the mark of Cain. "What is that you're playing?" she asked him in a hush. "The name of what that is?" she asked him again quickly. She hadn't even known to call it an instrument, a musical instrument, but her mother was already drawing her away by the sleeve of her dress. How could someone whose hands were so completely employed be a danger to her, but her mother then grasped her entire wrist and yanked her away. "It's a beauty, idn't it," he called after her. "It's a concertina," and his deep resonant voice carried down the sidewalk. "My mother played it and she gave it me when I was about your age."

She had thrown her elbow out against her own mother's arm and pulled away, knowing she'd pay for this later, but she could then look back at his long slender fingers against the burnished wood cutwork of the fingerboard, and she could see the leather handles across the backs of his dark hands, the leather shiny as oil. "Concertina," she had pronounced and he said, smiling gently, "yeah baby, that it, concertina."

The pillows piled one atop the other, her underpants drawn down, and his belt across her bottom as the immorality and emptiness of the world were lashed from her, and she saw the long dark-fingered hands working the buttons and heard the concertina music and knew the white, veined hands behind her wielding the belt, and she made her choice in a quiet closed space of her mind as her mouth screamed and her eyes sprang angry salt.

Earlier in the gallery she'd singled out the four black speakers in the upper ceiling corners from which the music sounded, and now as the gallery emptied it seemed that perhaps the volume needed to be quieter, or perhaps different music. She watched as the woman hunkered down, attempting to work

—

the key in the strip of stainless steel that ran along the bottom of an otherwise unadorned slab of thick glass that was the front door. The woman had nothing by which she could pull the door toward her, or hold it, but finally the key worked, and then she rose up and turned and looked straight at her, concerned.

"My name's Arabella," the woman said, walking toward her, and then she stood on the other side of the table.

"May I serve you a glass of wine," she asked the woman. "I've gotten pretty good at it, and I don't seem to be burning for eternity."

"What?" the woman said, her face tipped, puzzled.

"It's what I was told about alcohol, that I'd burn for eternity if I touched it."

"Charming thing to tell a child."

"I don't really believe it. I saw people drinking beer in Jedro's Wagon Wheel and they seemed like they were having a good time. Laughing, carrying on."

"Where was this?" the woman asked quietly.

She wiped the table with a paper napkin and lined up the bottles yet again, the white wine and the red wine and the water. She had already replaced their caps. She thought to herself that they were the straightest lines of bottles in all of Santa Monica. She knew that if she answered this question, she'd be telling the woman named Arabella something that placed her within a past geography. Police stations could be called, state services.

"I got away from there," she said.

"Yes, I think I see that."

"Do you want this all put some place else?" she asked. "In the back?"

"Isn't someone worrying about you?"

"That person died," she said. "My grandmother. Maybe she isn't worrying about me now."

"I see, okay. No one else?" Arabella asked.

She didn't answer, and she felt very suddenly exhausted, the image of her mother in her mind's eye, moving slowly about her kitchen, making her father his dinner, a skillet sizzling on the stove. Her father would no doubt be sitting at the table, rattling the ice in his tea glass, wanting more sweet tea, not asking, just rattling the ice in his empty glass as though that was the only way to ask for more tea. He would not waste his words for something the women should have seen he needed. He liked a glass full to the rim, and now she was sure that her father had already gone out to the back stoop and had broken her dinner plate, too, the way he had when he'd disfellowshipped her grandmother. "She no longer sits with the righteous," he had said, smashing her grandmother's plate across his lifted knee, and now her plate too, chipped, always chipped, as long as it had been hers, was also shards about his black shoes, the glazed blue flowers scattered, freed to the dust and to the hot sun that in the morning would find this tentative mosaic across the porch's boards.

"What do the red dots mean? The red stickers?" she asked Arabella.

"That means I did pretty well this evening!" Arabella said, tossing her head so that her beautiful black hair did that thing

—

135

of sliding like a wing across her face and then away. "Very well, indeed. Let's count. Three big canvases, and all of the drawings."

"So, they're sold?" she asked. "You sold the paintings?"

Arabella didn't answer but walked to a small table near the entrance and picked up a packet of papers and brought it over to her. "This is a price list," she said, "and each painting or drawing or whatever, sculpture, is listed with a price. Sometimes information about the work, and usually an artist bio somewhere, who's collecting the artist, museums, shows, but not always. So, collectors pick up a price list usually and walk around with it, or sometimes, in this town, it doesn't matter what the price is and a collector just points. Red dot time! Did you ask him your question? About why he put a time on his paintings?"

"I didn't know which man was the artist."

"The biggest fucking asshole in the room—you didn't see him?" Arabella looked down at her, amusement in her eyes. "You don't have much of a sense of humor, do you?" Arabella asked, slapping the price list down on the table, teasing her, she knew this, but hearing the impact nonetheless as admonishment, criticism.

She wanted to say the word "asshole," that Arabella didn't know what an asshole was if she thought any of the men here tonight, standing about on these polished cement floors, drinking wine from plastic cups, talking gently—if she thought any one of these men was an asshole . . .

"The man who stood over by the door to the office," Arabella was saying, "in the long linen duster, that was the painter—and watch, in a few years, when he's a little more famous, he'll paint that duster and sell it for some outrageous price. Fine, if I get to sell it, his tribute to Jim Dine, fine, but he's not all that talented and my sense is his star will rise and fall almost within the same year."

"That doesn't matter to you?" she asked.

"What doesn't matter—that he's not a good artist, that his work won't last?" Arabella threaded her fingers about the necks of wine bottles. She lifted three in each hand and walked to the office, the bottles chiming brightly. "We'll just have to see," Arabella said coming back around the doorjamb. "I always buy some insurance, a few pieces from the artist that I keep tucked away, pieces I feel show the early promise, pieces that might be raw and uncalculated, and which I can buy for almost no money because he or she is still unknown. So they're not the best work, or later, more crafted work, but they're not juvenilia, either."

She reached for bottles, too, tucking them in her arms. She didn't trust her fingers to pick them up like Arabella had, and then the table sat cleared of all but the paper napkins, a short knob of plastic cups. She ran the word "juvenilia" around her mind. She knew the word juvenile and so it wasn't such a reach, and yet she didn't know what this might mean with respect to painting. "Do you have some of his juvenilia here," she asked.

"Look around," Arabella said, throwing her arms wide, laughing.

"No, I mean—I guess I mean—the pieces you bought earlier? Do you have those pieces? Could I see them?"

—

"Yeah, I do," Arabella said, and her voice sounded suddenly serious, interested in her. "You really want to understand, don't you? Come."

She followed the black dress, watching the hem that she had sewn, the small stitches that allowed the hem to be more supple, to move more fluidly. Arabella stood at huge double doors so seamlessly flush with the wall that she hadn't really seen them. Arabella pulled one of the doors open, its header moving just beneath the ceiling, and then Arabella disappeared. "Would you mind clearing the rest of the table," Arabella called, "while I find these."

She held the napkins and the stack of plastic cups as Arabella reappeared pulling two canvases behind her on pieces of toweling. "Early Giamatti," Arabella said.

She noticed immediately that there were no times noted on either canvas, and that instead of buildings and skyscrapers and billboards, both paintings were views through windows into empty rooms, one with shadows on the floor and the other cast in bright light. "They're not even signed?" she asked.

Arabella tilted the one canvas away from her, and then she could see the signature on the back. "Does that matter?" she asked. "If it's signed on the back versus on the front?"

"Not really. As long as you have authentication. It's called *épreuve d'artiste*. I actually have pictures of these in his apartment where he was painting at the time. Yes, there are people who want anything hanging on their walls to advertise who the artist is, but with serious collectors authentication is what matters. I don't have enough cash," Arabella said, "to pay you for tonight, for your help."

"It's alright. You didn't ask me to help—I just did," and when Arabella turned to replace the paintings into the depths of the huge closet, she moved into the gallery and gathered her backpack that now contained bottlecaps and napkins and moved oddly with a quiet clattering against her back. She meant to slip away, to push through the door as she had this afternoon, and to be away by the time the woman Arabella looked up, but the door was locked and she hunkered down and struggled with the key at the base of the door and then Arabella was there, standing over her and she smelled Arabella's nylon stockings again and her perfume but then sea air and car exhaust because she had gotten the door open.

"Wait," Arabella called after her. "Please wait," but her white tennis shoes moved her down the sidewalk, brisk and fleet.

Lucille was ninety and being operated on. No one was happy about it and no one thought it was a good idea, but the tumors on Lucille's left breast were external, and the size and look of peeled plums, and now even Lucille wanted them removed.

On Friday, during pre-op, a nurse pulled Lucille's gown down to place an electrode for an EKG and the nurse had gasped. In contemporary times few have seen breast cancer let go this far; few knew breast cancer as anything but a detected lump deep down in the gelatinous flesh, but Lucille hated making a career of her health and handed people their heads on platters if they gave medical directives. Lucille went through doctors as though she was thumbing through the Yellow Pages. Lucille would make her own decisions, no matter how ill advised. Nine months ago a doctor had prescribed anticancer drugs that caused a precipitous decline in Lucille's mental and physical capacities, and now that Lucille was off them completely, and back to her vigorous if difficult self, she wasn't chancing her health and particularly her mind to blood-pressure medication, or to any other drug for that matter. *Of course I have high blood pressure*, she'd scowl, *I'm ninety years old. You think you get to my age without something wrong with you? Don't be inane!* Anyone trying to speak to Lucille backed off and smiled a little. It was curative to everyone to experience a completely sane and fierce woman of ninety fighting them all off; it was also frustrating because Lucille didn't seem to make distinctions between those who were there to ensure her independence and those who would addle her mind with drugs and scrub their hands of her. But now, now even Lucille was willing to submit to the surgeons. After the EKG, when the niece—recently in from Los Angeles—had posed some questions to the medical technician, Lucille had barked at her niece, "Don't ask questions. I'm in full possession of the facts: I'm going to die. Do you really need to know anything else? You inherit the silver."

Now it was 7 A.M. on Tuesday and Lucille's niece sat alone in the Day Surgery waiting room of the second story of Memorial Hermann Hospital in Houston, Texas. It occurred to the niece that putting "memorial" in the name of a hospital seemed an unfortunate harbinger, and perhaps sent a mixed message. Or not mixed enough.

The niece was waiting for the surgeon to finish and then come down the long hall of polished linoleum to tell her how the cutting had gone. The anesthesia was a regional block of the neuromuscular impulses that fed the area with blood and the anesthesiologist from Sri Lanka hadn't been sure just how much the surgeon could excise before the conservative anesthesia stopped working. Lymph nodes and some of the connective fibers of the breast—could the surgeon with her concerted hands cut out any of this without causing too much bleeding, without killing Lucille? The anesthesiologist had been shaking her dark worried head. She didn't like the high blood pressure. Couldn't they wait a few days to perform the

—

surgery; couldn't they medicate the high blood pressure, get it down, and then operate?

As more and more people came and sat in the waiting room, the murmur of voices mounting, the niece thought of the many discussions and deliberations with the many doctors, all of them women. The surgeon, the anesthesiologist, women, and the doctor nine months ago who had prescribed the disastrous anticancer drugs, the oncologist, a woman. The niece didn't know what to make of this, other than to note it. It had come over the news recently—and she had remembered—that over 50 percent of entering classes in American medical schools were now women. But the niece wondered if Lucille would be less hostile if her attending doctors were men? Lucille's behavior seemed increasingly furious, unchecked by propriety.

The niece, an escrow officer, had gotten herself extricated from a fairly busy schedule of openings and closings in Los Angeles and had flown down, first to Dallas/Fort Worth, then into Houston Hobby Airport on a smaller aircraft heaving and bumping through scudding clouds. The niece hadn't been on a plane in ages, nor taken a vacation, nor read a book, for that matter. On the flight, she sat a little stunned at her inactivity, delighted and fearful at once. She and Lucille were holdouts in a family riddled with cancer, and Lucille had no children. They had each other—though with a few parched states in between for whatever distance it was that so many American families seemed to need and desire. The niece had married and been happy, and then had lost him too, to cancer, as though he'd been taken into the family business. If her Aunt Lucille died, the niece held the entirety of the family's history, in escrow, she mused, a kind of permanent limbo because she had had no children either.

A teenaged girl was wheeled into the waiting area by her father, who hunkered down briefly and then rose with a massive and well-thumbed paperback novel with dragons on the cover. He placed it in the girl's lap and then without saying anything sped down the hall, peering right and left, looking for a restroom. His daughter leaned a little in her wheelchair. She was dressed in a pink sweatshirt traversed here and there with a network of thin chains and crosses. This odd chatelaine seemed some part of her novel's world, the world from which her eyes never seemed to lift after she'd opened its cover.

The niece sat thinking about doctors and about Lucille, but she was also reading a small novel by another old woman, one who had been a Stegner Fellow at Stanford when she was sixty-eight years old. This novel, the writer's first, had been released when the writer was seventy-four. These were the claims on the book's back cover. Inside the covers, the village doctor has just committed suicide, and the conjecturing of the two Americans who live in the little village of Ibarra is that the young Mexican doctor was sorrowful over his thwarted music career, and yes, it's his music, but it's the village, too, its backwardness, mothers refusing polio vaccines and crippled children because of this, and necklaces thought to cure pneumonia and herbal plasters on malignant tumors.

The niece liked the novel well enough but kept tenting it down over her thigh and gazing out across the shiny hospital floor. Lucille hadn't pasted mint leaves on her tumors, but for all of Lucille's intelligence, for all her beautiful patrician will-fulness, her refusals of medical advance over the years didn't now come off as sophisticated. Maybe the true challenge of old age was its inherent foolishness, no matter what choices one had made or not made. An old woman alone fighting to stay alive, and why, for what reason?

"You know there's coffee now, honey, you could get yourself a cup," said a woman walking toward the niece, a woman in purple shorts of the same fabric as her purple sleeveless tee shirt. The woman—holding with both hands a white Styrofoam cup—was trailed by another woman, younger but a hundred pounds heavier. This younger woman wore a huge sleeveless shirt that at first glance seemed to reveal the top of her huge white brassiere, but which proved on closer view to actually be a design detail, a yoke of white cloth. She held a Styrofoam cup in one hand and her fuchsia-pink iPhone in the other. "Mama," she said, "this coffee's goooood."

"I know," the woman in purple said to the heavy woman trailing her, "that's why I thought I'd tell this lady waitin' like us. Honey, who you waitin' on? We're waitin' on my son," and the woman didn't pause to let the niece answer. "My son's hav-ing a stent put in his heart. It's the drugs, you know, he did himself a lot of drugs when he was younger and now he's payin' the price."

"He's payin' the price," echoed the younger woman, settling her cup on the small side table, her attention drilled down into her iPhone. "He sure is. Before me, when he was with that bitch

Courtney, he did all them drugs. I know, I know, she's your grandbabies' mother—two of your grandbabies at any rate—but she's still a bitch, and a slut, too." The younger woman spoke without looking up or addressing anyone in particular. "If she'd satisfied him, he wouldn'ta done so many drugs."

"Courtney's still married to him, though, that's why I have to be here," the mother explained to the niece, "'cause I'm the next closest of kin and Violet here can't make no decisions 'cause she's just his common-law wife and Texas don't recognize that."

"Oh," the niece said, nodding her head, "I see. Really?" she then asked. "Texas doesn't recognize common-law wives?"

"That's what they tell us. I suppose they know. I'm sorry to sit so close, but I wanna plug my phone in there," and the woman reached her bare arm into the corner and settled the phone charger into the electrical socket and then took up her coffee again. "I'll show you some pictures when that phone gets up."

The niece nodded, rather thrilled to have these two women distracting her, entertaining her in fact. They seemed to know without her saying a thing that she wasn't from around these parts, though when the niece had packed her case for Texas, she'd selected clothing that looked formal and conservative by a Los Angeles eye: the clothing she saw on Saturdays as people walked to the various synagogues in her neighborhood, and also concomitantly, the clothing worn by the large, church-attending black middle class of Southern California. The niece supposed—marveling—that she'd rather subconsciously packed her church clothing, though her attendance at events of a religious nature was sporadic. Presently, sitting in the Day Surgery waiting room, she wore half of a pink linen suit, the jacket, embroidered with white leaves, and pearl earrings and their matching necklace of a pink cast all above slim jeans and pink Italian flats stitched in such a way that they looked arty and Moroccan. She didn't think she stuck out like a sore thumb or anything, but she and the two women who sat near her, talking to her, were the only three women without crosses dangling from their necks. She hadn't noticed this at first, but she kept wondering why these two women felt immediately so comfortable with her. Texans were friendly, easily so, "thatta fact," they'd say, definite, nodding, "yes sir, we're friendly folk," but the niece didn't think it was just that. Sizable crosses were in vogue with the rock-star set and two or three trendy clothing lines had tee shirts that sported huge rhinestone crosses in a Gothic typography. Crosses as design detail seemed to have the day. It never occurred to the niece that the young blonde girl in the wheelchair with the netting of chains caught here and there with crosses might actually be religious, or was actually signaling a specific religious identity. It never occurred to the niece that these large pot-metal charms had replaced—with any meaning—the small gold crosses of her day. And yet somehow, before coming to Texas, she'd packed her conservative clothing. Then again, maybe what she'd been preparing for was a funeral home and arrangements and meetings with the management board of the condominiums where her aunt lived.

"I'm seventy now," the mother was saying, "so I show people

—

pictures of my grandchildren, but I do it on this here phone and that's because these grandkids keep me up to date. I need anything on this phone, I just call up some of my litter and they're there doing it before I know it. I got fourteen cats, too, but they don't program the phone, course, they so cute, though."

"Fourteen cats, really," the niece said. She hated cats, but after a certain number, cats became the measure of something else in a person, and so, interesting. "How did that happen?" she asked. "That seems like a lot of cats to feed."

"We call this one cat Wally because I'm at Wal-Mart with Tiffany and some woman's got a box teeming with kittens and course Tiffany gotta have one, oh Grammy, Grammy, so Wally come home with us and before I can get her fixed she pregnant, seven kittens she give me, seven, biggest litter I ever heard of and she a little itsy-bit herself. I just made a pallet and slept on down there with her, rubbing her stomach up and down, up and down like I'm going up and down the aisles of Wal-Mart, and six come out and I go away and fix dinner, my husband he's older than I am, and I come back and there's another one, just lyin' there like a little turd but I see it's a kitten. Never heard of seven in a litter, you? 'cause that's a lot of kittens and I know I gotta give some away but they're three months old now and so cute and Tiffany, well, she like kittens."

"How did you get the other six?" the niece asked, pulling her book from her leg and placing the bookmark at its center. She thought to herself that few novels streamed quite as alive as these two.

"Oh had them, darling, had them. I'm not sure I'd even

—

147

remember where I got them all. Fixed though, so no kittens for many years and mostly toms."

Her daughter-in-common-law leaned her pale girth across the arm of the chair and said without taking her eyes from her iPhone, "I can tell you where she come by the two Persians if you really want to know."

"You shush. You don't put my bidness to the street."

The daughter-in-common-law snorted good-naturedly. "Safe with me, Mama, safe with me."

But the mother went on, "I'm seventy now, but there was a time. My husband, he's older than me."

"You gotta get it where you can," said the daughter-in-common-law, shaking her head, "umm, umm. I'm not talking about no fancy cats either."

The niece sat delighted with these stories. It seemed to her that she hadn't felt delighted in years. A lover showing up at the door with two exotic cats in tow seemed delicious beyond words, hilarious, and somehow Texas, too, *ain't takin' my baby no flowers half dead already.*

"She don't know," the mother said, her eyes glinting onyx. She smoothed back her once-black hair though it was caught neatly at her nape in a plastic clam claw. The niece noticed how small and narrow the mother's hands were, and though the nails were unvarnished, they were long, perfectly shaped ovals of pale pink.

"You have beautiful nails," the niece said to the mother.

"But I got the arthritis," she said, holding up her two index fingers, which canted outward at the last knuckle, one pointing

—

right and the other pointing left. "My granddaughter's wedding come up and I didn't do anything for three weeks, didn't cook, didn't clean, nothin', my nails were so perfect. She one of my other sons' daughter. I have four boys, raised them all myself."

"She look good for an old broad."

"I don't aim to look like I'm missing anything at home."

"Never said you look hungry—never said."

An intercom called for the family of Joseph Morris, *the family of Joseph Morris*, but no one in the waiting room responded.

"Got myself just what I need for home anyway," the mother said, winking at the niece. "My own little machine. My own little electronical finger. My husband he don't satisfy me. We been married almost thirty years now, twice, cause we were divorced for about five in there. He older than me, but he love all my boys. Course he wuddn't around till they were grown, still, he love my boys."

"I love my little machine, too," said the daughter-in-common-law. "It go for just as long as I want."

"I don't have nothin' to do with how they are in the sack—can't blame a mother for that," the mother said, leaning over to the niece to secure her point. "He my son, but I didn't do none of that trainin', you know, that they gotta do on their own."

"No, of course not," the niece said, laughing. *She was laughing*, she thought to herself.

"He ain't no plate of sweet water duck barbeque, that for sure," the daughter-in-common-law said, never lifting her face from her fuchsia phone, "but he mine and I'll take him, and he

—

better not look no other woman in the face—I kill him—kill her, too." The daughter hefted herself from the chair, pushing forward with her fleshy pink shoulders until she stood and walked splay-legged into the broad expanse of polished linoleum toward the sign-in desk. She shook her head back and forth as she went, her eyes never lifting from her iPhone or looking up, *kill her too, no playin' around with what is mine.* Her arms stuck out on either side in order to accommodate her rolls of fat.

The mother watched and then turned to the niece and rolled her eyes. "Look like she doin' the chicken walk always, you gotta wonder, but they love each other, they do. Maybe she gotta hold so tight cause she looks the way she do, but I don't like talk like she got him on a leash, then again he need a leash, I guess, wild, wild, wild, that boy, and drugs, lordy, the drugs, but he met her and he don't do that no more, course they got two babies now, not babies so much, both teenagers now, Daniel and Tiffany, but he had other children before her and he did drugs then so who knows, but she hold him tight, too tight, talk big all the time, kill this, kill that, don't like it none."

The niece tried to formulate something to say about holding someone tightly. She wanted to say without too much desperation tingeing her words that the daughter was right to hold the son tightly, but that she should trust him, too, and then the niece realized that perhaps the son hadn't grown up with the best model for marital fidelity. The niece didn't know, she didn't have any high ground, in fact her guy was long incinerated to ash and if she wanted to think about sorrow, regret, it would cluster painfully around not having held tightly enough, not having taken greedy possession of every possible moment with him.

The family of Lourdes Garcia, the intercom called, *family of Lourdes Garcia please come to the Day Surgery Sign-In Desk. The surgeon is waiting.*

"Do you have trouble with spraying," the niece asked after the ceiling had quieted. She would keep to the subject of cats. She didn't like them and she wouldn't spiral into sadness over them. She calculated that it would be an hour longer before she was called, *the family of*, but if the operation was going poorly, or if they were having to change Lucille's anesthesia from local to general, it might be much longer. The niece could conjure the worried face of the anesthesiologist, her dark ancient eyes in her elegant young face. The niece wanted to communicate with her, to send her a message that all would be well, that Lucille was going to come through, that nothing the surgeon or the anesthesiologist did or was doing now would harm Lucille. Of course, the niece didn't know this, and yet she did. Lucille's cancer wasn't the niece's husband's cancer, that violent raging replication within a much younger body. Lucille was ninety and her cancer for the most part had been sluggish, painless. Plus, the niece knew Lucille, and the Lucille she knew wasn't dying here amid beeping machines and faded hospital gowns and plastic cups. If Lucille had to die, and Lucille knew she did, though she most certainly did not want to, then she would do it amid her Federal antiques, her china, her Meissen cachepots, their perfect violets.

—

The ceiling called the family of Curtis Simpson, *please come to the Day Surgery Sign-In Desk*.

The niece hated the way cats smelled and ever since she'd heard "fourteen cats," her nose had been full of it. She'd had homes fall out of escrow because of cat spray, and sometimes entire hardwood floors had to be ripped out and replaced before an escrow could close. "The cats, I mean," the niece said now. "Don't they spray?"

"Just about everything," the mother answered. "Particularly if it new—toms always gotta spray it—new couch, chairs, mark what's theirs. SPCA say they won't spray after they do free fixin', but toms is toms. Smell pretty bad."

"What do you do about that?" the niece asked.

"Nothin' you can do. Four or fourteen, don't matter the number, still smell bad."

Fourteen cats, the niece thought to herself. Fourteen reeking cats, doctors operating on a ninety-year-old woman fierce as a snake and awake! Whoa, the niece thought, Whoa. Amazing what people signed on for.

The niece had known a little of what was in store for her in Texas, too. She knew all the many charades of control in the face of the big closing in the sky. Her thoughts were not without bitterness. She knew a little about being alone and at the center of the great fracas. In her small bungalow in Los Angeles on Hammond Lane, she had packed, folding her clothes quietly and laying them in the narrow black case. She had watched the flame of the candle she'd lit, the silver picture frame behind it reflecting the votive's flickering—the flickering all around his

—

smiling face, the most pleasant of men, kind, sweet, and somehow the other end of the spectrum for him, pancreatic cancer, the most rabid, painful of cancers.

"You don't want no coffee?" the mother asked. "Pretty good." Her daughter-in-common-law ambled back from the Day Surgery Sign-In Desk where she'd been standing, talking to the clerk with her shining black East Indian hair.

"They still working on him," the daughter-in-common-law said, "but we can see him when they finish and he wake up."

"A Rest and Wait," the mother said, and both mother and daughter-in-common-law laughed loudly.

"What's that?" the niece asked, knowing she was hearing a phrase that meant something specific.

"Oh, that's what the police call it, they stop you and you mouthin' off at them or mad and shouting, acting out, they just let you sit. Put you on the curb. Rest and Wait. Good thing, too, since Texans take to their guns."

"We got our guns, that's for sure, but I wouldn't pull no gun on no cop," the daughter-in-common-law said, "that'll end you in a mess of trouble."

"Any state you're in, that's not a good idea," the niece offered.

"Seems like everyone spoilin' for a fight these days, itchin' to use their guns," the mother said, finishing her coffee, the white Styrofoam cup squeezed into screechy collapse in her hand.

The niece wanted to say *itching for a fight in Texas*, but she couldn't really isolate that to Texas, that sense of people just ready to strike, all of us snakes in a way, coiling in preparation.

—

What was that about? Richest country in the world, freedom probably about as much in evidence here as it could realistically be anywhere in the world for a human animal, yet people mean and getting meaner, except, perhaps, these two women who had chosen her to talk to, chosen her among the several other people spread out in the waiting room. Then the ceiling called her name, *the family of*, and she rose quickly from her chair, almost bumping the mother's legs, apologizing to her as she placed the novel behind her on the seat cushion. The niece felt she wanted to save her place in this huge anonymous room in which people waited to be identified as family, waited to be brought forward into proximity with the powerful, the technologically adept. The niece moved toward the Day Surgery Sign-In Desk, but already the doctor in her long white lab coat over pale green scrubs stood just a few feet away, pulling her surgical mask farther down off her chin. The doctor smiled, relief on her young freckled face. She turned and walked the niece across the broad hall to a far wall. "It went as well as it possibly could have," she said, "but I didn't remove anything other than the external tumors. There was already a lot of bleeding."

The niece felt the surgeon looking at her, gauging her reaction. "Okay," the niece said, "I understand. How long do you think before they grow back, or before others grow?"

"It won't be the breast cancer," the doctor said, leaning her shoulder in against the wall. "She's metastatic, you understand—"

"Yes, I know, the cancer's in at least three different places."

—

"It will be the cancer in her throat," the doctor said, smiling sadly. "That will probably take her. Nine months maybe."

"I understand," the niece said. She was used to closing dates, to hearing them set down, agreed upon, and she was comfortable being between parties, a guard against both and a protection to both, but this was different from her work. The dates were only surmise, hesitant pronouncement, a begrudged inevitability, and whether or not her aunt should be guarded and protected and just how or what that might mean, and whether or not she even wanted that!—this was nebulous, too. "Nine months until the tumors grow back, or nine months until she's dead?" the niece asked, persisting a little, but she knew her question was senseless, that it couldn't be answered, that it put the doctor in a terrible position. The doctor could charade about, could make a stab at predicting the future, which is most often what people wanted of her. Or she could stand aside and eschew this false authority.

The doctor hesitated, unsure herself which route to try. The niece and the doctor both knew the doctor could throw a lot of language at the niece and probably the niece wouldn't try to surmount it, wouldn't try to dig her way through to question the doctor further. The doctor could cow just about anyone with her knowledge, her training; she could even lie, make it up, medical-sounding gobbledygook, and the doctor'd be out of there on to her next patient, a tall gooseneck faucet cascading purifying water over her sudsy hands, the medical assistant holding a new chart up to her to read: *invasive lobular carcinoma; biopsy shows microcalcifications* . . .

—

Finally, the doctor, pulling her mask completely off, said, "She's very strong, you know—we all know that—and she's fighting, but I would venture she has less than a year. The first tumors we were able to shrink but others grew twice as fast as the original ones."

"She's not going to have her way with this, is she?" the niece said, her eyebrows raised at the doctor. She was trying to signal that she understood. "Strong as Lucille is, she's not fighting this one off."

"She'll probably be an hour or two longer, just resting," the doctor said. She smiled wanly. "And then she can go home."

The niece now held out her hand. "You've been wonderful, Doctor, thank you."

Perhaps because they both were women, because they'd been talking about the care of another woman, a very old woman, palliative care, this resort to professional etiquette, the shaking of hands, seemed strange, silly, beside the point. The surgeon looked down at the niece's extended hand, a hand similar to her own, small and capable, without rings. It seemed to them both a long float of time, and then the surgeon pulled herself up from the wall that she'd been leaning against. She switched the surgical mask to her left hand and then took up the niece's hand and shook it quickly, deftly; she was a surgeon after all, and she'd withstood what it took to be a woman training to be a surgeon, and she shook hands—or could shake hands as vigorously as the next guy, but this was all a holdover, the niece suddenly realized, an act of a former time, *take my hand that holds no weapon*. When had women really been a part of that anyway, toting around swords and daggers and pistolas!? Pretty much the surgeon didn't need to indicate to the family of the woman upon whom she'd just operated that she wasn't holding any weaponry—why on earth were they participating in this ridiculous exchange of the obvious?

"I'm sorry," the niece said. "I'm sure you favor your hands, like a musician does. I guess I'm always trying to make sure people shake one another's hands," but the doctor had already turned, her black rubber-soled clogs squeaking quietly down the broad, polished corridor. The niece stood motionless, watching the narrow back of the surgeon in her long white lab coat, its hem moving stiffly above the legs of the flimsy green scrubs. The niece watched until the doctor turned left and disappeared. Then the niece raised her right hand to cover her heart and bowed slightly from the waist.

A movie perhaps? a meeting between heads of state, one a woman, the other a Muslim man, was that why they didn't shake hands, didn't touch? or was this just the way heads of state greeted each other in peace these days? No transfer of infectious disease for them? Where had the niece seen this etiquette performed? The hand on the heart, the bow. The niece didn't know, didn't remember, and she felt mortified that someone might have just seen her do this ridiculous thing in an American hospital in the midst of Texas. The niece didn't know whether she was mocking or had been serious, some subconscious emergence of behavior she'd seen and had now adopted? What was the etiquette of the contemporary world? And when that question was settled, What did one wish of it?

—

The niece returned to the waiting room. She had no answers, she thought to herself, and glancing up, she saw her novel on the seat cushion, its cheap paperback cover canted up into the air. This image seemed to her simple and human and somehow silently distraught. But she saw what she wanted to see, saw the image in her mind's eye only, because her novel wasn't there, where she had left it to keep her place. Nor was the mother in her purple cotton jersey shorts and tank top, nor the huge wonderful manatee of a daughter-in-common-law with her pink iPhone. How quickly the niece had felt akin to them, their company, how quickly she'd wanted to return to their banter and familial play. God, did she hate even the idea of those cats, but that's what being a family is, loving what on certain days you hate, but they weren't there to love or hate, to be encompanied by.

The chairs weren't empty. The man was perhaps Chinese, his wife Mexican or Guatemalan, a Latina, and their child sat where the niece's book should have been, his small round face still and worried and subdued. The niece wondered for a moment, tonsillectomy? a small hernia in his little groin? Perhaps it wasn't even he who was the patient; perhaps it was his mother? What prospect held his small face so quiet? And then she heard herself being called, "We're over here—we have your book!" and the niece looked up and into a deeper area of the waiting room in dimmer light, one lit lamp on a corner table, and the mother waving the thin paperback book, gesturing *over here, over here*, and by the time she got across the shiny hospital floor, mother and daughter were already talking about something, something the daughter-in-common-law thought about how good one of the other son's wives had it. "Always greener on the other side of the fence, I guess," the daughter-in-common-law said, laughing at herself, her brow raised, her plump face intent upon her fuchsia-pink iPhone.

"Green where you water it," the mother said, *green where you water it.*

In the flat black wallet that had been her grandmother's was the one-hundred-dollar-bill that she would never spend, though she understood it would probably be taken from her one way or another, stolen or confiscated. She walked east, away from the ocean, her body barely catching in the dark store windows, her shoulders a white smear. Most stores were closed or closing and the grates rested halfway down, waiting for the last person out, for the final locking of doors, the switching off of the last lights. She walked along the vast lighted car lots of a dealership, and then along the marble lobby of an office building with a dark-suited guard sitting atop a stool at the entrance to the elevators. One of his legs reached to the white marble floor, the other was bent, propped on a stool rung. He stared into space, and she thought that if she could sit atop a stool inside his head she would hear him speaking quietly, to a brother, or to his mother, some-one perhaps dead. She could look out the glass of his eyes onto the street, the murmur of his conversation around her like music. She could sit upon a stool inside his head for a long time, she thought, but she walked farther down the sidewalk, becoming a little warmer. Billboards glowed above her in the night sky, car insurance and expert senior medical care, and then that same billboard became Small Animal Hospital of Santa Monica and then Ralph's Grocery Stores. Electronic billboards, she said to herself, though she did not know what they were called. She walked, and occasionally caught the white of her tennis shoes moving beneath her, the white a little smudged, a little dirtier but for the most part white, an invitation. A series of buildings began that seemed to be hospitals or medical offices and she wondered if she might be able to walk into the lobby, the pretense of visiting someone, a family member hospitalized, *I had to work, but I got here as soon as I could*, she might say to the person at the reception desk, her grandmother was here being taken care of, lying in pristine white sheets, smiling when she pushed through the curtains, *about time you got here*, her grandmother might say. . . . *Did I ever tell you that method for pickling radishes?*

She slung her backpack from one shoulder to the other, she slung off the fantasy, the child's play of her mind. Toys, she said to herself, Don't make toys in your mind, brightly colored useless plastic toys, and she scolded herself. Scolding kept the pain down in her chest, kept the tears away. Her grandmother was dead. She did not know where her grandmother's body lay, and it certainly was not here in a fancy hospital in Santa Monica in pristine white sheets.

She walked. Buses and cars coursed along the broad boulevard, brakes sounded, the occasional horn. Stopped at a light, a black sport utility vehicle reverberated with pounding music behind its blackened windows. The traffic lights released cars and curtailed them, released and curtailed, and for a while, she took up the challenge of meeting cars at the next light, walking very fast, and then slowing, waiting with the cars, and then taking off, walking fast again, but then she would lose a set and need to choose other cars, the couple playfully arguing

—

with the windows down about how fat Godzilla was. "Since when are monsters sleek and fleet of foot?!" the young woman exclaimed, and he was laughing and seemed to say, "Well, why not." She ran after this car when it took off, her backpack thumping softly against her back. She wanted to hear them more, to laugh with them. She didn't know what Godzilla was, other than a monster, but they both obviously loved him, or was Godzilla a her, maybe so with that *a* on the end of the name, but then coming up to the car, she heard, "It's a fucking alpha predator—you want thin!?" and then their laughter, and his "Yeah, a set of tits, too."

She was warm now as she walked, and exultant and not so afraid as just freed into this city and its intricate expanse. She saw a billboard across the street, glowing within the night sky, the huge words "Salem" and "Witch Among Us," and a girl's face in profile with bundles of sticks protruding from her eye sockets and from her wide open mouth. A hemp rope cinched the girl's neck and beneath the translucent skin of her cheek and shoulder was a network of veins as though she had been under water for some time. At the top of the billboard a raven or crow perched on the sticks in her eyes. "Sunday, April 20, 10/9C."

Witch Among us. This was what was done to women who worshipped Satan rather than God, or God's son? She thought this was a television program being advertised, but it seemed so much a piece of almost any sermon she had ever heard, the punishment awaiting her if she disobeyed her father, disobeyed his Father, God. She looked more closely at the rope around the girl's neck, and she was a girl, really, this "witch among us," with the coiled knot of a noose just below the uplifted chin. She stood with her hand on the back of a bus-stop bench, staring across the street at the billboard lit in the night sky. The sticks protruding from the girl's eyes would have to have been pushed out from the inside of her head because of the way the skin of the eye sockets flushed outward. So, she thought, by hanging her, this girl who they thought a witch, by hanging her what got forced from her mouth and eyes, forced from the inside of her head, was twigs and small branches, perches for ravens and crows. The girl's mind was a home for birds, she said aloud to herself, her mind gave birds a place to land, to perch. Fine then, she thought defiantly, my mind will be a place where birds come, where birds come and make their nests and feed their young, fine, in my mind birds will sing, fine, choke me and my eyes and mouth will vomit sanctuary. She was screaming and she looked around to see if she was screaming, if anyone could hear her screaming, and she knew her rage for the many times her face had been hit or slapped, rage at the hand flying at her, no raven, no crow, her father's metal hand. It would never fly at her again. Only birds could come there now, her mind a tree, and from this tree—open-winged—they would fly.

—

To tell them from the drinkers, the drug takers, the compulsive fornicators—it was not hard. Her office window in the rectory looked out across the courtyard, and she kept the sash raised just high enough to hear and she watched through the wooden slats of the Venetian blinds. She saw that the stances of these lean men as they waited for their meeting with the Father were directed outward, looking anywhere but at one another.

On Tuesdays there were five men, on Thursdays six, and their exchanges, if she thought them exchanges, which she didn't exactly, seemed perfunctory, clipped, the little that had to be said between them just occasional flickers of sound in and around their silent understanding. Language was the way by which they were held accountable, she reasoned, or by which their "debts to society" were deemed paid or provisional; it was noise to the side of them or behind them, necessary for others perhaps, but not, it would seem, for them.

These meetings on Tuesdays and Thursdays were a compulsory part of their registration, their probation, and they were less a group, less a collection of the like-minded, than they seemed to her drawn together against their will toward a goal they did not recognize and for which no amount of keening by others could incline them.

She decided those minutes just before their meeting began would be the time when she would take the Father his afternoon coffees. The men gathered around the short flight of stairs at the side of the church, their gazes dropping to the ground quickly, anxiously, or pointedly alert and preying, the unrepentant among them. They had beaten women for different reasons, good reasons, defensible reasons! That had all started with language, too, women's words, their ability to wield them—how their words chiggered themselves into you!

From the rectory she walked the path between the blooming azaleas, a small chased tray in her hands, and each meeting day now she wore pieces of jewelry she'd bought from the department store's ground floor, rhinestones and bright metals, and she came to look as though she were a face in a window of costume jewelry, so much so that Father Purdon commented on Tuesday:

"Eliza, perhaps you're drawing the wrong attention with that much flash. I know it must be dull for you here, but evenings might be a better time to don those accessories, hmm?"

She hadn't said anything to the Father's hmm. She was not the one who had brought these men among congregants on the church grounds, these men who tossed their cigarette butts down and mashed them beneath their shoes, or drilled them, still lit, into the bushes. She thought that all manner of accommodation had been made for their rich crimes, and yet she was to temper her attire. Azalea, she thought to herself as she walked the path today, the Greek word *azaleos* means "dry." Her Greek was good, her Latin excellent. "Azalea" because it grew in dry soil.

She held the small tray in her hands today, and a long thin

knife for the lemon bread she had made for the Father's after-noon pick-me-up. The loaf's sugary glaze had clouded to a glaucous opacity making the loaf appear as though wrapped within a caul. The knife jutted up from her right hand. She was holding the knife this way so that it didn't slide from the tray and clatter across the flagstones; she was holding it this way so that it could be seen, so that the blade would perhaps even flash in the sunlight.

She remembered putting on her lipstick in a fine restau-rant once not so long ago, holding a silver knife horizontally as a mirror, her pale face, the bright red lipstick, the wattage of candle flames reflecting in the knife's surface. "Are you ready?" her date had said to her, his hand beneath his lapel, feeding the long leather wallet down his breast pocket. Then that small action was complete, as was his smile. "You see," he began, "you do all the breathing for the room and that's a big responsibility. We'd all die if you let us. And you let us die all of the time."

She had laughed; she thought it was a joke! She thought it was a great compliment, the love of female beauty—How they waited upon it! What it drove men to do! How grand!

"You resent that so entirely, don't you?" she said, laugh-ing, turning her back to him so that he could drape her shoul-ders with her coat, so that she could feel his hand at her neck, pulling her hair out from her collar. It had taken her years to understand what he meant, years to understand the resent-ment. And now her life within the embarrassment of her faded face—there could be no sympathy for that. It was like asking them to admire impotency.

—

He had seen the knife, the lean man here only on Thursdays with his sharp jaw and the cropped hair, and the expensive, hand-stitched linen suits. He looked, his eyes drawn to the knife, and then he had looked past her, past the knife, and turned, his shoulders hunching and stiff beneath the fine fabric. She wanted one struggling to hold onto himself, fighting himself. One like that would be easier to work up, and she had spotted him long ago, tender and venomous. She knew who had bought that suit. Not really, of course, but she had an idea. She also knew that any *she* would do for him, she knew that, too, as she met his eyes and then she let slip the knife, hoping, oddly, that it would not slice her hand as it fell to the ground.

Perhaps she heard it hit more loudly than it did, but he turned and leapt across the short distance of walkway and bent and retrieved the knife. Now she could smell the wood and leaf of his cologne, and she saw out of the corner of her eye the sharp angularity of his jaw as he trailed just behind her down the long flagstones to the back of the church. The deep afternoon light darkened beneath the tall old trees and he reached the tray from her hands and set it down beside the door to the Father's study. He held the knife close against his pant leg, and they walked along the parking lot with its few cars and into the small woods beyond. Oaks and rhododendrons and elms. Her rhinestone earrings caught the dulled quiet light. "Does she buy all your suits?" she asked, "choose your socks, too, your shoes—"

If she regretted the first stab in her side, just beneath her ribcage, his other hand at her neck, she did not know this, nor

—

did she feel the furious retraction of the knife in order to drive it into her back, nor the knife's retraction once again in order this time to lean over her slumped body and place its point at her heart and then to place his polished shoe over the hilt end and stomp it in as though it were a tent stake—if she regretted anything, it was that she had waited so long, had fought so hard against this moment.

She looked at the bright shine of the knife blade driven into her chest. She saw the knife she held as a mirror in a fine restaurant, her lipstick glistening.

—

He didn't like her, his next appointment. Her dyed-blonde hair, her gums receding, making her front teeth appear bigger, broader, the beaver look. He didn't want to hear about how the last crown he'd put in her head didn't feel perfectly comfortable yet. He'd saved her tooth, for God's sake. They all wanted the teeth of twenty-year-olds! Their iPhones and iPads and they wanted new eye teeth, too! New iTeeth! Hah.

He was sitting in his office, just off the waiting room. He wouldn't make her wait, there was no reason to do that, and yet somehow he wanted to like her more before he led her into one of his two operatories.

"Hello, Doctor," she called, as though she was happy to be there, waiting in his waiting room, chipper even about having her teeth cleaned, but he didn't want those comments about the last crown, the suggestion that his work was not up to snuff, and yet professional protocol would compel him to ask, "How is that crown settling in?"

He leaned across his desk and turned the Scarlatti sonata up just a decibel or two. The scalers and probes were out of the autoclave, and the set-up tray was complete, and he'd laid a dry-back bib across the chair. Did he need to smile as he asked her? Would a look of dire concern be better, even if dishonest? He was one of the best crown men in the field and he still did most of a tooth's contours by sight, but she was a grinder, a bad

—

169

one; her teeth took a beating every night. He feared they would always hurt her.

"How are you, Doctor?" she went on. "Are you ready for me, or no? I'm perfectly happy here with the new *Sunset* magazine."

Then again, he didn't like most of his patients, or were they clients? He wasn't sure what paradigm was in vogue these days. The twenty-first century—had it left him behind? or had he declined to enter it? Of course, the twenty-first century was happening to everyone, was happening around the world, and yet America perhaps loved it the most. Was it all just a financial transaction now, a product they were buying, or did he still have some responsibility beyond fee for service? When he'd kept a front desk staff, they would have known, "client" or "patient," which word, they would have kept him current, but they'd left long ago, and he worked the desk now, let the voice mail handle the calls, and in between appointments he returned those calls, settled the date book. There was more and more time to do this, and because there was, he talked himself into the quiet, staffless office. Didn't need them anyway.

Occasionally he would wonder, Had his staff left? Or had he run them out? Patients asked at first, Where was Norma? Cindy? Are you on your own today, Doctor? But no one said anything anymore. No one asked. It was the economy. It was hard times, or perhaps it was just computerized times, which helped lead to hard times. Everyone just knew, or answered in their own way, why there was no longer someone to greet them, to bill them, to fan out before them a colorful selection of toothbrushes, this office's tradition, a new toothbrush a visit . . .

—

but everyone just knew the Why Not, and that hush of not saying what was on everyone's mind prevailed, an enervated pall,
hardly enough charge to even ask the bigger questions: Where
was all of this leading? What had they done to their country?
Whose fault was it?

He supposed it had started with the sign in his office against
cell phones, the sign that came about because he'd been working on a patient's teeth and his cell phone rang and the patient
had waved him off, saying, "I need to take this." He, the dentist, was to sit there on his castored stool, Gracey curette in one
hand, mouth mirror in the other hand—and wait? Maybe they
were customers now and customers were in charge? It took a
couple of cell phones being answered as he worked before he
added a charge to the patient's bill for his wasted time. When
he'd drawn blood once, because the patient sprang up to answer
her phone and his curette had cut her gum—then he had put
the sign up.

"Are you ready for me, Doctor?" she called again, quietly,
and then she said, in her contented way, "I'll just read until you
are. Happy to do so."

He heard the couch in the waiting room, the dull huff
of her weight on the old foam, the couch that was now, once
again, cutting-edge design. All the museums in Los Angeles
were suddenly gaga for Danish Modern, and his waiting room
could be an entire installation—Installation! Everything from
the knubby upholstery to the long-armed chairs and the low,
acute end tables. Los Angeles County Museum of Art, the
Getty Center, MOCA, the Geffen, for their purposes—Art

—

and Design from the Sixties to the Eighties—they could have
lifted his entire office into one of their galleries. Even his philo-
dendron looked original and remarkably like the one in the
Charles and Ray Eames living room at LACMA. There was
a time when his office had been at the vanguard, its waiting
room design by Hans Wegner, the side tables by Kurt Østervig,
and the layout of the operatory, its pale blue equipment—even
his X-ray pale blue—and his dentist smocks, which he still
wore, pale blue, with a wide zipper up the front. He had had
one of the first videocams for kids so that they could watch
what was happening in their mouths, view their baby dentition
being pushed out by the mature. He could teach them what
a molar was way back there, a bicuspid, an incisor, a canine
tooth, but kids now came fully loaded with entertainment and
watching the dentist work on their cavities didn't interest them
much. Not even the drill that made those cavities fillable stayed
their attention for more than a second.

In truth, no children came to him anymore anyway, and
though he'd always been made nervous by the hovering mothers, he also thought he'd been good with children, instructive,
friendly and calming. He'd been the dentist they didn't cry at.
He knew that's where he'd been at his best as a doctor of dental surgery. With children. He had a funny round head with
funny round eyes and children immediately knew him as the
prototype of someone on their own playgrounds, skinny, with
delicate long-fingered hands, who wore eyeglasses and whose
voice was several batsqueaks higher than any other boy's, and
somehow children, with their intuitions, malicious and other-

wise, knew he wouldn't hurt them, wasn't capable of hurting them, was the opposite of the school bully.

But the children didn't come any longer, and because he'd gotten tired of fighting with the insurance companies, he'd taken himself off the lists for the various dental plans and so those patients didn't come either, nor the referrals from those patients, and then his patients of long standing would die—so many people died. No one had ever told him in dental school that he would struggle to preserve teeth, tend them year in, year out, keeping them in optimum condition and that one set would be shattered as the bumper of a huge SUV came through the window at her, his patient, or that another set would be turned to gray mush by a drug the FDA had no qualms about allowing on the market, or that another set would disappear entirely, his patient scuba diving through underwater caves in the Yucatan. What would the anthropologists in twenty thousand years think when they found that mandible with its perfectly capped teeth? What would they read from the metal alloys and the porcelain, all man-made? It would tell them nothing about diet or weather conditions, none of the facts that anthropologists could tell from early hominid teeth—what those teeth had gnawed on or ground up. The scientists sure weren't going to find a diet of sedges and grasses, and they weren't going to be able to figure out Coca-Cola either, though perhaps they'd find traces of phosphoric acid? Fossil remains. Late-twentieth-century diet was not going to be kind to future scientists, he thought, and the twenty-first century would be no kinder, with so much happening within those little electroni-

—

cal boxes that were obsolete and unreadable in three years, let alone three thousand.

"I've never gotten used to Christmastime being citrus time," she called. "Then again, it is, so what are you going to do about it!" She laughed. "You always have the most recent *Sunset* magazine. Such beautiful pictures. California in December."

Why was she going on and on, he thought, and then he felt desperate. One of the few patients he had left, a good-humored patient even, and he was resenting her. He rose from his desk chair and walked through his office door and emerged in the hall that passed alongside the reception counter. He would ask her calmly, gently, How is the crown feeling now that it's been in place for a while? He would ask her if she's had any other tenderness—he would get through this appointment and the next, but standing there on the counter, next to the pen in its holder, and his business cards in their low bowl, was a bright red foil-wrapped Santa Claus. Perhaps the Santa was eight inches tall. He looked at the high round belly girded with a broad belt and a black buckle. It said See's Candies. She had brought this chocolate Santa into his office. She had set it upon his reception counter. "Oh," he said at first, surprised, "how cute," but then he just couldn't. "Why?" he asked. "Why would you bring this to me—I'm a dentist."

Her face above the *Sunset* magazine appeared carefully. "You've been my dentist for so many years," she said, "and I just thought—"

"No," he said. "I've closed my office. I should have called you."

She stood up, still holding the magazine open to its colorful pages. She looked at him without saying anything, and then she turned and leaned down to place the magazine back on the Østervig end table. When she faced him again, she ventured by way of words and tone to ask, "You wanted to say goodbye to me in person? I think I understand." She said this kindly.

"You'll have to find another dentist," he said.

"Okay," she agreed quietly. "Do you have a referral, somewhere I can have my X-rays sent?"

He didn't know what to say to her. It was like trying to speak to the dead, or to the not-yet-born. Somehow he'd been left speaking to no one, to no one alive. All those years tending to the one thing that remained of a human body, all that preservation and care for the future, when what seemed wanted was the new and expendable. It was another century, and he had no one in it to refer her to. He held up his arms, his palms out. He could have been a laughing Santa Claus atop a roof; he could have been Jesus.

—

"I have never quite seen anyone screaming like that but not screaming," the woman said to her, patting the bus-stop bench, patting it to say, sit by me, and then the woman spoke again, " 'If you don't have anything nice to say about someone, then come sit by me,' " and the woman patted the bench again, laughing.

She didn't want to speak to anyone, and she didn't want to stop, and yet she had been screaming, or not really screaming, but this woman had seen her, seen something in her face. The woman smelled powerfully and the stench made her stomach flip over, and the woman continued to murmur, *Come sit by me, come sit by me, ain't got nothing nice to say about someone, come sit by me*, and the woman laughed, her shoulders in their several sweaters shaking. "Know who said that?" the woman asked her, looking across at her. "You don't," the woman announced. "You don't know at all. None of you know anything. Dorothy Parker—and even when I tell you, you don't know who that is, do you?"

"No," she answered, "I don't know who that is." She settled her backpack on the bench and heard the quiet chatter within of the bottle caps and screw tops. Something had kept her from emptying them at the art gallery and now they moved in her pack as though animate, an accumulation of something, a beginning, items that said she understood what a bottle of wine was, a beer, mineral water, "Bottled at the Source." She looked down at the woman's pale white face, delicately boned, fallen.

"None of you read. You don't read a thing."

"I don't have anything to read right now," she said, still standing. She could not settle beside this smell, this stench.

"I grew up in Port Arthur," the woman said, "my daddy, he worked for Gulf as an engineer. He'd come home and sit in his big chair and he'd call me over—I was three or four years old—and he'd say, 'Baby, Baby, come sit on my lap,' and I'd scramble up in my white dress with the lace collar—those days girls wore dresses like that—and he'd pull out his big gold pocket watch and hold it to my ear and say, 'Listen, Baby, listen, hear the little nigger chopping wood,' and I'd listen chop, chop, chop."

The woman sat quiet for a time, her head slumped to one side, as though she were a child again, listening to her father's gold watch. Then the woman stood up and walked around the bus-stop bench and crossed the sidewalk and then pulled from a dark doorway a huge blue suitcase on wheels. The woman wore jeans that had once been blue but were now black, and a wool kilt skirt over the jeans. Her feet were bare and filthy and abscessed as though rotted fruit, and the woman rolled the suitcase across the sidewalk and then struggled to pull it between the bench and the street. Barely enough sidewalk for its girth, but finally the woman managed and then the woman laid the case down and unzipped it and its canvas top flopped into the street, the zipper glinting in the streetlights.

—

She counted four rows by five rows of paperback books. She thought they went perhaps two or three deep.

"I can spare you one of these," the woman said to her, "but you need to promise me you'll read it. I was brought up with manners. You start a book. You finish a book. Then you return it to the person you borrowed it from if you don't own it."

She started to laugh, thinking the woman was being funny, but then she wasn't sure, and so she held her laughter in check. She wanted to leave, to continue walking, to find some place for the night, or perhaps just to walk through the night. She wanted to leave the smell of this woman, a smell so pungently layered and ripe it drove it home to her that she might smell this way herself soon if she didn't find some place to stay. She realized that she was scared of this woman in a way that was very different from the way she was scared of doing the wrong thing in the gallery, or of Julien Stoke when he'd found her searching his mail. She knew she could be this woman in a matter of days, filthy and sort of crazy and sort of not. This last frightened her the most, this in-between. It was what her mother was, conscious but unable. She thought it was probably better to be completely crazy if one was letting oneself go, to recede so far behind the wall the stench built that no one could come near, could come over that wall. She took from her backpack her grandmother's handkerchief soaked in Florida Water, and she held it close to her nose and yet she did not think the woman completely insane.

"I guess I've only ever read one book," she said to the woman now, "and you're not supposed to ever finish it, or be without it."

—

The woman murmured something beneath her breath that she couldn't understand. She waited, thinking the woman would explain or would go on, but the woman didn't say anything more for a time, her face gazing across the street. She couldn't see what the woman was looking at, and then she realized the woman wasn't focused on anything, it was just her gaze peering off into the distance, but then the woman finally asked, "You have that book now?"

"No," she said. "I left my Bible behind."

"That's too bad," the woman said, "because it's a very useful book for all these other books."

"It is?" she asked seriously, but the woman was waving the bus past. "Don't stop here, you fool," the woman yelled. "I'm not getting on, and neither is she. You aren't, are you?" the woman snarled, turning a furious bird face at her.

She stepped back from the bench without knowing she was, without intending to, the force of the woman's anger pushing her off.

"Where does that bus go?" she asked the woman. Perhaps she might take a bus somewhere, she thought, a ride across a greater distance in this city of distances.

"Westwood. Century City. Downtown. Staples Center. Japantown. Convention Center. Koreatown. Koreatown before it gets to the Staples Center—"

"Okay," she said in order to stop the woman. Maybe the woman would have named places all the way back to Barstow and Needles. "How much does it cost to ride the bus," she asked the woman.

—

"That's not interesting enough for me to know," the woman replied. "That's the type of thing you find out on a gadget— you'll need to get yourself one of those." The woman smoothed her hands down the tops of her thighs all the way to the hem of her skirt, getting more and more agitated. She thought the woman could be forty years old, or sixty, or even eighty. She couldn't really tell, as though something had been removed from the woman's face by her illness, some accounting of years removed and replaced with storm and confusion, outer darkness, miasma. "*Anna Karenina*," the woman said to her. "Have you read that? If there's any book a young girl should have read by now, it's *Anna Karenina*." The woman folded her torso completely down so her head was drooped between her legs and started to sort through her books, moving them around as though they were puzzle pieces. Ultimately the woman held a thick paperback book in her hands without a cover. "Here," the woman said, rising and shoving her in the shoulder with the book. "Go off and read this and fall in love with Count Vronsky and then never in your own life do anything as stupid as that."

She wanted to laugh again. She thought the woman was funny, but she wasn't sure, either. "I'd need to return it," she ventured, not knowing exactly if she was operating in a real world in which the woman expected her to return this old paperback book, or whether the woman would forget she had ever sat on a bench with a girl who had been walking down the street one night in Los Angeles, a girl whose face she had seen scream without making a sound.

"Come on," the woman said, leaning back down to her case and running the zipper back around. "I'll show you. You need a place to stay tonight?" she asked.

"Yes, I do."

"That's fine," the woman said. "You can bide with me."

"Port Arthur's in Texas, right?" she said to the woman's back as the woman started away from the bus-stop bench dragging her suitcase.

"You don't seem to know much, but you know where Port Arthur is. How's that?"

"I guess I did have another book, now that I think about it. It was an atlas and it lived beneath my grandmother's bed."

"That's where you lived, too," the woman mumbled, "beneath the bed."

They walked to the corner and turned down a side street and then turned down another, the wheels of the suitcase thumping quietly behind them, and then the woman gestured at a small, clapboard cottage beyond dense trees. A car stood in the driveway covered in brown leaves as though in camouflage. She could see that it had not been driven in a long while. The woman raised her hand and pointed adamantly at the cottage, her hand moving furiously, mechanically.

"This is where you live?" she asked the woman, perplexed by the fervor of the woman's gesturing. She watched the woman's small hand fly at the night as though it were a gray bat or a wadded piece of paper launched into the dark, and then she looked away. "It may take me a little while to read this," she

—

said, knowing she couldn't enter this house, couldn't be near the woman's smell much longer, nor sleep within the shabby clutter she knew would be beyond the front door. She saw the white immaculate walls and surfaces of the gallery, and the simple concrete floors polished into something that looked water-slicked but permanent, rooms with so little clutter they felt calm and coolly responsive, like being housed within a breeze. "I'll bring your book back," she said to the woman. "Soon," she added, "I'll bring it back soon," and she stepped off the street curb and walked briskly back toward the streetlights of Santa Monica Boulevard. She needn't have hurried, she realized, looking back. The woman stood unwinding loops of rope from her gate, the huge suitcase containing books standing behind her on the sidewalk, a dark blue sentry, sturdy as a dwarf.

The bodhisattva stood on the top shelf of a metal stand placed catercorner in the small humid room infused with camphor and lavender. I stood on the floor just inside the door, my blistered feet comfortable at last in black flip-flops four sizes too big, inhaling the vapors. I wore a beige waffle-weave robe and was naked beneath. Pain burned across my neck and shoulders. The bodhisattva glowed a Frigidaire white and had a long electrical cord that decanted down the wall to the socket. I didn't have a clear mind on these things, and not on Buddhism in particular, but didn't the much-sought nirvana have something to do with the extinction of the interior self? The subduing of the senses?

I looked at the precision of this glowing bodhisattva's resin moulding and heard in my mind's ear, "Man, he's really lit," my cousin's appraisal of the groom at the wedding we were all in Colorado for. There had been three evenings already of Texas line dancing and the Texans in the family were being Texans, whatever that meant to them, and "lit" seemed the required state of drunkenness for being able to throw one's dance partner across jutted hips and up and over shoulders and down between the legs. The bride and groom were as lit as necessary, and I thought the "lit" was impressive, indeed, as were the outsized dance moves. I wasn't sure it had much to do with inner peace, but maybe I was reading those Texans all wrong? I didn't know, but there was such an outward insistence on big that I surmised it might signal something constricted on the inside, big state, big hair, big makeup, big hats, big rifles, big trucks, and it all shouted a kind of moral meanness that seemed electrified by fear. What the hell were they so afraid of?

The events thus far, the chuckwagon cookout on my uncle's ranch, the fancy get-to-know-the-families dinner at the Strater Hotel, the rehearsal dinner hoedown, had been lousy with cops, guests of the groom's father, huge beefy-faced men so giddily a stereotype they seemed cut from comic books. Who—I mused—was fool enough to confront these guys, spoiling as they were for any outlay of physical power, though I supposed "outlay of physical power" a particularly absurd and decorous way to phrase what amounted to violence. I'd been treated to one drinking session in which a "man wasn't a man" till he'd beat the shit out of someone, et cetera, et cetera, and I felt pretty sure this was also a crowd in which "women weren't women" without dropping a few babies, but the babies seemed mostly proof of virility as I didn't hear much about the love of being a father. I was happy to be wrong, in fact would joyously be wrong, but just try having a discussion about the wisdom of abortion in certain instances or the sovereignty of a woman's body—I'd slap down a few shots of tequila for that exchange— but I was on standby for these events, held away from any true exchange because it just wasn't "nice" to think any differently than these keen protectors of our nation's highways and byways. Holy fuck did I need a massage, and the wedding hadn't even happened yet! That wasn't until later this afternoon at five and

the festivities would no doubt comet on into the thin hours of
tomorrow morning.

I'd gone to graduate school in Denver and during ski season
each year a joke got retold, or even after a while just alluded
to, as everyone knew it, a punchline that went something along
the lines of "If God had wanted Texans to ski, He'd have made
bullshit white." Remembering that line, my chin jerked a bit
in amusement, and it had seemed true, the Texans hotdogging
wildly, even down into the bunny slopes, blading dangerously
close around toddlers dumped over on their wee skis. Many a
mother looked up and yelled "asshole" at their flashing backs.
I had never wondered until now how anyone on the slopes had
known they were the Texans. But late in the day when people
had stood their skis up in the stands and gathered in the lodge,
there were the same flashing backs yelling their drink orders
in their gruesome accents across scores of people waiting. Texans, and then there had been the fake Texans in the White
House, all told twelve years of them, but they were originally
from Connecticut and educated at Yale. No matter, it seemed,
as Texans were welcoming to outsiders, at least they were that,
big embracers of the like-minded! My cousins were transplants,
too, and now born-again Christians, or reconstructed believers,
or some kind of UNDER NEW MANAGEMENT banner they now
stood beneath.

 It would seem that I was presently up close and family with
a few of these Texans.

—

I had tried to be a good sport, to dance when I was asked at the chuckwagon cookout and the hoedown just last night, but my strain was manifest on the dance floor set up in the pasture just down from the house. Let's just start with the fact that I wore dresses, and though we were out under a blueblack mountain sky, I was being thrown back over someone's knee and so when my dress hiked up—as a dress will tend to do when its wearer is catapulted—I gave a peepshow no one had paid a quarter for, nor did I assume anyone so inclined. And because this activity—some called it dancing—is oh so full of vim and vigor, just when I was getting my dress settled back down around my thighs, my hip bone would be slammed up against a belt buckle as though being struck by a truck grill. The first time this happened, I said, attempting understatement, "Perhaps you could soften the impact," but my partner's face was impassive with concentration: he had an old heifer on his hands. Then there was the common dance maneuver of being thrown into a straddle on a man's thigh, and maybe I was just a dirty-minded middle-aged woman, but honey, come on! You want to be up my crotch that far, fine, but let's call it for what it is, the Texas Line Dancing Dry Hump.

"Pardner," I said, thinking to attempt the vernacular, "maybe some lubricant before you try that stunt again," but of course, I didn't say that, I said instead, "Plates of meat."

"What?" my partner yelled, the roll of his hat like a prow jutting from his forehead.

"Feet," I yelled, because although my high-heeled shoes usually treated me kindly, I was asking a lot from Italian slingbacks on a dance floor in a cattle pasture. The straps had gone to war on my ankles.

He smiled broadly and I could see that he thought I'd said *What a feat*, and *Neat*, as though I was impressed.

What happened after a while when I held my tongue is that my body forgot where I'd put it, and when I did try to speak—no matter what I was trying to say or respond to—the words tumbled out, garbled and halting. Holding my tongue made me stupid, intensified my boredom, but I was turning over a new leaf in my life, attempting to slide right on through certain family events without snagging myself up on what would amount to a few months of extenuated, though real, guilt about having spoiled some family dinner, having confronted some righteous remark.

I was trying hard not to engage, as my aunt had requested, struggling to just let comments sit on the table as though they had squatter's rights, now owned the land, weren't goin' nowhere. During the last few days I'd risen from a chair more than once, risen so quickly I was sure people thought I was about to wet my pants, but I had to earn something. What I'd bought myself before driving to Flagstaff and then up to the trading post at Cameron to Tuba City and then across that long hot desert stretch of Black Mesa and on into the small town of Ignacio, was a 1920s bracelet and earrings from an estate jewelry store in Los Angeles. A bribe, sure enough, something on my person that settled me in its beauty, fourteen-karat gold set with old pieces of red coral. The Iranian woman had said, her English exquisitely accented, the bracelet draped across her narrow hand with its manicured nails, she'd said, "Coral like this is impossible to find now—red like this today—they've dyed it." The woman let me pay installments, laid it away for me, and now the bracelet and earrings sat wrapped in a velvet pouch in my cosmetic case a room away. I had already worn them once, to the dinner at the Strater Hotel in Durango, but of course this was a diamonds crowd. Diamonds, number 10 on the Mohs scale, the hardest stone, I kept saying to myself all evening, and coral was at best a 3 or a 4, and that was another aspect of my stupidity: coral was a less-than-stellar investment; diamonds were, well, for fucking ever.

As were tattoos, and I'd had a close call at the bar in the Diamond Belle Saloon of the Strater Hotel when a niece of mine—yet another one—had turned her lovely narrow shoulder to me, an aunt she barely knew, and asked me what I thought of the garden door snaked with vines and flowers covering one entire scapula. *Tattoos are so yesterday*, I'd started to say, *and incidentally, so forever, too*, but I caught myself. I fingered the soft red coral, feeling the bracelet around my wrist. I checked the gold backs on my earrings. My restraint was at least in place, if not magnificent, but also, unfortunately, I could not manage to get anything out of my mouth of an articulate nature, could not say *Oh, how striking!* or *How big!* or *How did you come to choose that design . . . by which the smooth plain of your entire beautiful shoulder blade has been graffitied?*

"What are you drinking," I finally asked, but my niece held

a martini glass in her hands with a pick of olives, and so looked quizzically at me. I then managed to add with the inflection of a question, "vodka or gin?" but even as the words came from my mouth I knew that if it were vodka it would have onions, not olives. Then again, perhaps that was unreliable now? Used to be you could read a tray of drinks, no straws were the drinks for the men, and the vodka martinis or Gibsons had the silver dime glisten of an onion at the bottom of the glass. Gin martinis had olives. God knows what they were floating in drinks these days! Pickled okra? Hot peppers?

My niece and I turned our silkily clad bottoms on our respective bar stools and faced the massive Victorian bar with its carved mahogany columns and its gleaming bottles. I felt a little stern, a little mean, and I didn't want to feel that way. I knew I came off that way to others, and when I both felt that way and was being perceived that way, I hated it. It made me just want to flee, to be alone, to come back to a place of gentleness.

"You always drink white wine, right?" my niece asked me, "and you always have fresh flowers in your house in Los Angeles."

I laughed happily, and though it used to be that people knew I was laughing with joy and amusement, now it seemed people thought I was laughing at them. "That's what you've heard about me?"

"Yeah," she said, looking down into her martini. "Other stuff, too."

"Oh?" I said, turning to her, my eyebrows raised.

—

She pronounced the words "you eloped" as if they were deliciously scandalous.

"Didn't elope," I said. "We just went away, did it alone, quietly."

Suddenly the saloon erupted into ragtime and we swiveled around and watched the piano man lambaste the keys. We'd gotten one good thing out of Texas, I thought, Scott Joplin. Know how they make a honky-tonk piano sound like a honky-tonk piano? I started to explain to my niece, but then I heard through the pounded chords, "Everyone says you eloped."

"Mis-use of the language," I said loudly, "and it's a shame, because it makes what we did seem illicit, and far less sweet."

Now I thought to explain to her that of course language was the way that others could own this event, by calling it something other than it was. I thought to explain this to her, too, but instead I said, "It's not quite as expensive as you might think. If you buy an orchid, a potted one, it will last two months, sometimes even three—that's what, thirty or so dollars amortized over several weeks. Not much for fresh flowers."

"Where do you buy orchids," my niece asked, putting her glass down on its small square napkin.

She seemed to be utterly serious. She practically had a compost heap inked onto her back and yet she didn't know where to buy orchids. "Almost anywhere nowadays," I said, "even grocery stores, but in Los Angeles, I have a place I go to, a Japanese family, and I take them the pots and they fix them up with moss." I laughed thinking about the plastic dragonflies they clipped onto the flower stems because they knew I liked them, but I could see that my niece thought I was laughing at her. "What I'm laughing at is that the old Japanese father knows I favor these silly plastic dragonflies, you know, they secure the long stems to the stakes, and he saves the green ones for me."

"You must go there a lot."

"Just every three or so months."

"But they remember you," she said.

"Yes," I said.

"I think I'm pregnant," she then said so quietly I was both sure and not sure that that was what she had said.

"Oh, sweetheart." I knew that out of a hundred and fifty people at this entire wedding extravaganza, my aunt and I were the only two people she could talk to without censure; I also knew that I might as well be the back-alley abortionist killing just as many young women as successfully bringing fetuses off others. She perceived me as someone she could talk to, and as the enemy. What a country.

"Do you want to come see me in Los Angeles—you could even drive back with me on Sunday," I offered. "We could have a long talk. That's what long drives are good for, long talks."

"I'm keeping it," she said, defense in her voice.

"Sure," I said. "Have another martini."

"Fuck you," my niece said to me, sliding from her stool, the martini grasped in her hands.

Perhaps what I should have broached was the possibility that tattoo ink was not all that wonderful to have in one's body, and that if a woman was planning on having children, it was probably safer to not inject one's body with ink, even if the ink

—

191

was just suspended subcutaneously, or at least theoretically it was just that. The studies—how much ink actually got into the bloodstream—were inconclusive, but nowadays a study of cars running over children turned out inconclusive, so who knows?

I managed a large clinic for women that provided low-cost obstetrical and gynecological care, and I had done so for fifteen years. Because we provided free contraception, I also controlled—as well as anyone could—our California press, followed reproductive issues in both the professional medical journals and in the national exchange, dealt with some of the stupidest people who ever used up the world's oxygen, and some of the smartest. Most of the rest of America sat some-where in between.

I looked at my niece departing through the swinging lou-vered doors of the saloon and out into the old hotel lobby, her tattooed door going through a real door.

"Nails," I said to no one. "They put nails in the hammers of the piano to get that tinny sound." I turned back to my wine-glass and took it up. The bartender had me in his sights, per-haps because I'd been speaking aloud, but he looked quickly at my glass, saw it didn't need refilling and looked away. "Ruins the piano," I said to him, but I had been disappeared.

My uncle was all that was left of an old Colorado family, or rather that old generation, my father, their parents and grandparents, old Colorado, with grocery stores in Rifle and Salida like store-fronts on a Western set at Paramount Studios. Those generations had talked about clabbering cream in bottles in the storefront

windows and five-hundred-pound sacks of flour and it seemed
to me they all used that phrase "just leave people be." A few years
after my father died, my uncle had come to L.A. in search of
me, said, "I don't need to lose my only niece," and though there
was plenty of the younger generations, I was one of the few who
knew the old, too, had sat with my great-grandmother and listened to her stories of cutting blocks of ice from the lake and
the train bringing in oysters from the east coast. She might have
even sweetly scoffed at oysters being flown in to Durango to
the Strater Hotel, "Ah, that's no feat," but 1910, fresh oysters packed in ice from the Chesapeake Bay, now that was
high-altitude derring-do. She wasn't nostalgic, and wouldn't
have let anyone else be. She told plenty of stories of maiming
and death, and she had had to hold a rifle on her second
husband, the one she'd married after my great-grandfather
died, the man who was supposed to be a father to her seven
babies. She had caught him skimming off the top of the till.
He might as well have taken food out of their mouths. She'd
once stopped a family dinner cold by saying that she thought
young people were very smart these days to live with each
other before they married. Just leave people be.

It was tradition when I visited the ranch, because of all the
natural hot springs in the area, that my aunt and I went for
massages, and this time my aunt—even with scores of people
wandering about and a wedding in the works—had not forgotten our ritual, and though she didn't have time to go herself, she
had scheduled this massage for me, and there had even been
half-and-half in the refrigerator for my coffee when I arrived

—

four days ago, and a bedroom for me alone upstairs in the ranch house. My aunt didn't forget me, tended to watch over me, even though she wasn't really related to me but had married into the family after my uncle's first wife had had the kids and then died, and the family talked about my aunt behind her back, thought her "stupider than a sack of stones," and yet my aunt seemed always to know where I was, or what I might like.

Now, today, a few blocks away, my aunt was getting a manicure along with the bride and the attendants, and still other women in town for the wedding had filled a salon just off Main Street in Durango. With all those diamonds, their hands, their nails, needed to look worthy, but my aunt knew I hated sitting that long without being able to do something with my hands. Four days ago, my car shuddering down the dirt road in its approach to the ranch, my mind going over the things I enjoyed about coming here, I'd assumed there would be no time for the hot springs and this hour of comfort, but when I arrived and one of my tall male cousins had taken my bags from the trunk of my car and walked them up the stairs to my room, there, on my bed, on the log cabin quilt, was my aunt's note saying "Deep tissue massage, 1 p.m. Saturday. Prairie Gentian Spa, my treat, love you, mean it!"

SPA was my acronym for remembering the historical sequence of the philosophers Socrates, Plato, Aristotle. I didn't much tell people that because it tended to garner incredulity, but it mattered to me that it was Socrates who had never written anything down, had insisted on speaking his thoughts and then because

—

he didn't necessarily hold by the current God-ery in Athens, had been made to drink hemlock, and it mattered to me then who had listened to Socrates and written his words down and then who had come along and naysayed whom, and why. I liked that Socrates' mother had been a midwife, and that Socrates used the idea of midwifery with respect to helping people come to knowledge. Or maybe Plato had used the metaphor for Socrates? I didn't remember that now with any kind of precision, but this seemed forgiveable to me just as long as I knew vaguely the early roots of democracy, even though Plato pretty much loathed the idea of it, of mob rule. At the same time, or rather in the same course, I'd studied logical fallacies, of which there were about eighteen or nineteen, and these I unfortunately remembered with some precision, and this sometimes made living with the opinions of others rather difficult.

I stood now in the small, becalmed room hearing for the first time the chime-y music, Asian and synthesized. I thought it was probably an ethnic slur to call this sound Asian, and I missed the actual quiet of my simple Korean spa in Los Angeles, but in this instant, I had not one complaint as long as someone touched my body with the intent to relieve.

For two days now I'd entertained myself by helping put replica Conestoga wagons together for centerpieces, and last night I'd spent four hours tying ribbons on one hundred and fifty miniature cowboy hats that had had the audacity to arrive with their hatbands missing. My cousin the bride swore the picture of these adorable wedding favors had shown each hat with

—

its own tiny cord. The absence of hatbands seemed to blow gale-force disappointment across the bride's smooth young features and so I'd quickly volunteered my nimble, bored-to-death fingers. I was a serious little worker in a clutch, but I wasn't sure that anyone save my aunt credited me as such. I was an egghead of sorts, in effect the enemy, someone who thought about policy and women's health, about privacy, and diamond rings weren't my interest, and had never been, and this last really made me suspect. Nonetheless, I would happily fetch ribbon and get to work.

"Oh, but what color?" wailed my cousin the bride when I'd posed this conundrum before getting in my car and driving to the nearest town for ribbon.

"Well, what color were they in the picture?" I asked, looking up into the young woman's unhappy face.

"Pink," my cousin the bride said sadly. "They were pink."

"Always a good color," I said before someone hooted out that no self-respecting cowboy hat had a pink hatband.

I refrained from suggesting that these darling itty-bitties were made in Taiwan and self-respect seemed an American tradition of the past. Finally brown—Brown!—was settled on and before I could say *Would that be Wedding Brown?* I happily folded into the air-conditioned hush of my car, rolled it quietly off the grade from the ranch house, and set off for Aztec, a town about forty miles south and sure to have a store of some kind. I took with me a bag of the tiny hats just in case my car broke down or I blessedly ran out of gas and could sit by the side of the road, smelling the sagebrush, tying yet one more ribbon hatband around a small plastic crown.

All of that to say my back was a mess, but I felt rather proud of the hundred Windsor knots I'd accomplished before remembering he'd taught me how to tie a Prince Albert, too, which was a sort of cleaner-looking knot and less bulky. Bows on the tiny cowboy hats had just not looked right—even I had that much of a Western aesthetic.

There was a timid knock on the door and I said, "Come in," and the masseuse peeked her serious young face into the room.

"I'll give you a little time," the masseuse said. "You can hang your robe on the back of the door and lay facedown on the table."

"You can stay," I said. "I don't need time to do that," and I watched the masseuse's face take on a kind of confused horror.

"Oh," the masseuse said, pausing, "if you're wearing a bra and underwear, could you—"

"No, I'm not," I said, knowing I was already in the thick of it, but tired of it, too, and now suddenly—or perhaps not so suddenly—willing to just clear the room of stupidity. "I'm getting a massage," I said. "I'm not wearing anything under my robe—why would I be?"

"Oh, okay, yeah," the masseuse said, and her blue eyes were careful and excited. "You know. Some people are very modest . . ."

"Yes, I've come to forget those people," I said under my

—

197

breath, though not quietly. I started to shake the robe from my shoulders, feeling the chaff of its coarse, baffled weave down my back and across my arms.

"I'll give you a minute," the masseuse said quickly, pulling the door closed.

"Oh, for God's sake," I murmured, letting the robe fall into my hands and turning to find there on the door as promised "a hook by which I may hang my robe" I intoned to myself . . . sure enough, a stubby white plastic elbow-macaroni of a hook and placed to accommodate giants. How thoughtful. I half-tossed the robe's neck up the door, and then grabbed it as it slid down. I stood on tiptoes, my arms stretched up, fumbling the thin fruit-loop onto the slippery round plastic point and then my jaw came back on me and my breasts and nipples were being touched and I realized the door was being opened. I thought to say "Just a moment, please," but then decided I'd just move back from the door and begin my ascent onto the sheeted table. I supposed somebody modest would be scrambling, squealing to show the true depth of her modesty, sliding as quickly as possible beneath the sheets and blanket, her eyes closed at the horror, the horror of the nude female body! I was convinced this was shame, not modesty; I wasn't interested in participating. The door closed quickly this time, almost a slam and so I took my time sitting down on the table and lying back and then flipping myself over to wedge my face down into the outhouse hole of the massage table, or was it a horseshoe, I asked myself, a padded horseshoe for good luck. Oh God, did I need this, I breathed.

—

But I had begun to worry about receiving massages—about the masseuses. I'd seen a television program with masseuses being interviewed, telling stories of vomiting after giving a massage, of taking into themselves some person's anger or violence as they worked the muscles, of feeling filled with horror or sorrow, or rage, having to leave the room crying. Of course, it took a particularly sensitive, particularly empathic masseur or masseuse to pick up trauma, to perceive the images, too, but one of the masseuses being interviewed had seen in her mind's eye a horse's neck geysering blood. It turned out that the man whose back she was working on, his father had missed with the pistol as he put down his childhood pony. Another masseuse had severe cramps as she massaged a woman who'd recently miscarried her twins, and the masseuses supposedly hadn't known these stories, hadn't known the people whose bodies they were massaging.

Mr. Park hadn't been able to touch me six weeks after my husband's death. "Pain," Mr. Park said in his heavy accent, pulling his hands from me after just a minute, then lowering them and trying again. But I could not be touched and my whole body flinched even though I'd received acupressure massages from him for years. He then reached down with both hands and lifted my shoulders from the table, pulling me up into a sitting position. He rested my head against his chest. With his upper arm bracing my back, he wrapped a towel around my wet hair and then he furled the white sheet around me and carried me to the terracotta room and laid me on the heated floor. "Stay here," he said, and I remained in the dense heat of the floor like a swaddled child, or like a body in a shroud. Then an older Korean woman came for me.

"Not too long," the woman said, helping me up. "Mugwort bath, okay now. Then go home. Go home. Take care."

There had not been any question of charging—they wouldn't take my money that day—and the two Korean women at the desk had looked at me carefully, the obsidian shine of their eyes just that, dark and shiny and presuming nothing but knowing something. "Take money back," they said, and I hadn't known whether they were warding me off, warding off some darkness I'd brought into their lives, or whether it was just simply business, unfinished business that couldn't be paid for?

It was now so many years after his death and yet, for about four months now, I had had a series of images flashing in my head, the bathtub filled with blood, and blood on the walls and floors and on all my scarves and small purses in the drawers beneath my vanity. The images flashed and reflashed. I would be sitting having dinner with friends, and suddenly a match struck up in the dark cave and my mind exploded with the mayhem of the house. Images with no resolve, no future, like music stopped violently mid-note. There was a name now for the compulsive repetition of trauma, an acronym that rolled off tongues too blithely, too pat, and it began to mean nothing, or seemed so prevalent as to really not matter much. Didn't we all have something, some harm back there, didn't we all remember it too vividly? Didn't we all replay it over and over again in the huge and lonely theater of our mind?

—

In the Prairie Gentian Spa I wanted the masseuse to come through the door anytime already! But I feared her entrance, too. She seemed so young, younger than my many nieces, barely twenty-one, if that, and careful to the point of erasure, as though all of this attempted calm, this imposed silence, insisted on it, insisted on erasure. Maybe that was accurate to Buddhist precepts, I mused, the subduing of the self and of the senses? It was a kind of erasure, wasn't it, and it supposedly led to enlightenment, to self-illumination. I raised my head so that my chin propped itself on the table edge. The bodhisattva glowed in the room's dim light, and I laughed quietly. The self had to get beyond suffering, and when that was achieved, you were either extinguished, or you were "lit." I decided I needed about ten of these electrified bodhisattvas for Christmas presents. I looked at the room's one small window, the glaucous patterned glass high up in the wall. I felt immensely, expansively empty, as though a great desert went on and on within me, a reservation I'd been passed onto, torrid and vast. I was alone there. I would never be beyond it.

I hadn't had an acupressure massage from Mr. Park since that one attempt, over six years ago now, but I received scrubs and forty-minute oil massages from the women at the spa, and in the last months, I had watched their faces carefully, and every time now they were sad or looked exhausted, or cast their eyes to the side or down and did not look at me as they wrapped me in a white towel and sent me off to the steam room. They had known me for so many years, but in the last few months they had been different toward me. Was I making them sick now, too, sick with my anger? Earlier this summer, the FDA had further restricted the drug my husband had ingested faithfully, according to doctor's orders, the supposedly benign cholesterol-lowering medication Zocor. I was seething anew with rage, and trying also to survive on this vast scalding plain.

The masseuse emerged through the door so quietly, I barely heard her. I drove my face back through the padded doughnut and I felt her hands pulling up the blanket, smoothing the sheet across my shoulders. Her name was Cora and I had met her briefly at the front desk, her hair very long but very heavy and flat against her head, as though she'd been wearing a hat for two weeks. Cora. What an old name, I thought. The only Cora I had ever known was my Great-Aunt Cora, my grandfather's sister, and she had had that matronly heft of another time, another era, a thick solidity like a sack of flour in a suit and heels. Now women of that age were just all jiggly fat in tee shirts and lug-soled shoes. No wonder the young were terrified of getting old.

"Is there anything I should know," Cora asked me quietly, "anything I should pay particular attention to?"

The question took me off guard, caught me up. The Korean women never asked a question like this. Or any questions. The Korean masseuses smiled broadly, easily, bowed their heads. "Facedown," they all said, their hands held out, guiding you onto the table, and they wore black bra and pantie sets and no one else wore anything at all in the quiet steaminess of the baths. There were no questions. Occasionally a woman who wasn't Korean would give an instruction, a directive, but other than that it was massively, pervasively quiet, and their sensitive, trained hands seemed to know within a few seconds where the tension was, the fisted muscles, the knots clenched beneath the skin. *Facedown. Turn over. Other side.*

I didn't think I'd answer Cora's question, not because I was being difficult or stinting, but because the minute Cora touched my back and neck she'd know the answer. Instead, I asked her if she'd ever had to stop giving a massage? "I understand that sometimes you pick up rage or sorrow and that you have to take it into yourself as you give the massage—is that true?" I asked. "Has that ever happened to you?"

"I have a detoxification regime," she said easily, confidently. "Because, sure, you take a lot out of people's bodies."

Cora was smoothing my hair away from my neck, starting to work the tendons there. Her touch was too tentative, too soft, annoying. "Do you see things," I asked her. "Images?"

"Oh sure," Cora said, folding the blanket a very careful distance down my back. I sensed that she didn't really want to talk about other massages she'd given. She said to me by way of answer, "I understand you're in town for a wedding."

"That's right," I said. "A niece, who's actually a cousin, but you know how that happens."

"Tell me if I hurt you," Cora said.

"Your touch is so light it's not possible. I'm used to acupressure massage. You can't hurt me."

I was lying of course and I thought about this as the words

—

203

came from my mouth. I hadn't had acupressure massage in almost seven years. And as for hurt, it was hard to feel subsequent hurt, to sort it from the resident hurt—it was like saying you can't get me wet because I'm already submerged. So, it was true and it wasn't true. Still, if Cora continued to pet me, I'd scream.

"I start easy and then get into the muscles," she said. "If you start out digging at them, the muscles just tighten up more."

That made a kind of sense to me even though I'd never experienced any kind of deep tissue massage that started up gently. "So, you see things during a massage?" I asked pointedly, but Cora had begun to knead my right shoulder.

"I'm going to bend your arm across your back so that I can really get into the muscles—is that all right?" she asked.

"Sure," I said as she began to lengthen and flatten my body onto the table. Break it off, if you want, I thought, seeing my disembodied arm moving about by itself above the dance floor, my arm curved as though grasping a shoulder, and then my arm straightening, letting go.

"You don't look drunk," the Justice of the Peace had said, smiling wryly down from his bench. "You bring a witness?" He laughed at us shaking our heads, and he waved one arm at us, teasing, he'd sign as witness with his left hand and he'd sign as Justice of the Peace with his right, and we handed up to him our marriage license, which had had to stew for twenty-four hours in the little island town, or not stew, as the waiting was to ensure people weren't drunk. We stood in the paneled courtroom, its nineteenth-century wood a richness that contained

us, and we were frightened, sober, ecstatic, and we were setting off into our great vast future. The Justice of the Peace
was funny and we were now laughing and he groaned coming
down off the bench, walking around so that he stood in front of
us, his robes settling about his bare calves. He was wearing red
Bermuda shorts. The bailiff was summoned and he looked at
us disgustedly as he ambled across the floor and bent down and
signed his illegible name. The words "the noble estate of marriage" were spoken and then we both signed our names, one
arm laid across the other's—we wanted it done, we wanted our
release, we wanted our bottle of champagne, our small cake,
our room looking out over the dark Atlantic.

"I actually feel kind of giddy," Cora said quietly, finishing her
work. "Like I've been laughing." I lay on my back now and
her hands were laid across my cheeks, hot as two mugs of tea.
I started to open my eyes, but then didn't. I was under, perhaps
almost asleep, and the great planned event of my head, that
huge white marquee tent under which so much happened, had
quieted into aftermath, the grass trampled by so many feet, and
white napkins dropped here and there like magnolia blossoms,
and hundreds of glasses on the tables, and the music now silent,
but palpable still in the late darkness.

"So, it was okay?" I asked hoarsely. It felt odd to speak, as
though my throat had to delve deep down into a pile of rubble
to find the words.

"No," Cora said, "but you were laughing."

"Really?" I asked.

—

She laid her hands one atop the other across my forehead. "It's what I hear," she said.

I opened my eyes and looked up tentatively. I thought to tell her something, to tell this person with her long flat hair and her clear blue eyes, this person I did not know, that he used to say I was incredibly happy until about noontime, at which point humanity, its horrors, finally dawned on me. I could see him laughing, saying this, shaking his stately head with its beautiful hair.

I thought about lying in bed with him in the wee hours of the morning, all those intimate hours happy with advent, all that silky dark delight before the hot interminable day.

SHE

He will send forth His angels with a great trumpet and they will gather together His elect from the four winds, from one end of the sky to the other, she quoted as she walked beneath huge old trees, walked beneath the dark canopy of one to beneath the dark canopy of another, toward the lights of Santa Monica Boulevard. She thought of the Outer Darkness, that place where *there shall be weeping and gnashing of teeth,* that place here and now, where she was, *for many are called, but few are chosen,* for she was not chosen for heaven, nor had she chosen to be chosen. Car lights caught in her eyes and then passed and reddened, and then were white and bright in her eyes again, and then once again red.

She placed the thick paperback book on the bus-stop bench, and then flipped it over so that its back cover was on top, so that its pages wouldn't thrash in the wind. Except, she teased herself, there isn't any wind. She then turned east, away from the ocean, away from the few people she had met thus far today. She walked many dark, quiet blocks, one closed shop after another, shoe repair and Asian antiques and silver replating and nail salons, all dark, and then blocks as brightly lit up as daytime. She reached a freeway overpass, the broad littered sidewalk going under it reeking of urine. She smelled the night, full of stench, of fetidness. She breathed through her mouth, walking past the huge cement columns encrusted with constructions of cardboard and blanket and discarded chair, dwellings, she realized, hearing voices coming from within, from under blankets fluttered by human arms, human heads. Forts, she thought, like children might build, like she could if she had to, oh God, she thought, if she had to—though not here. She hurried, terrified, without running, the sound of the bottle caps and screw tops murmuring at her back, *"Get away from here, away from here," and she had* and she was now *away* as she emerged from beneath the overpass into brighter darkness, into constellations of car lights.

She crossed streets of four and six lanes of traffic, crossed within the dense mechanical indifference surrounding her, swallowing her small sounds, and she saw through windshields tilted expressionless faces lit by cell-phone screens, and then her own face surprisingly in a panel of mirror on a glazier's truck. There you are, she thought, her dress looking limp and flimsy about her legs, the wide straps of her backpack dark along her shoulders, and there you aren't, she said to herself, forging on, this image already a she of her past. She heard her grandmother's voice explaining how to dress meat, game, venison, opossum, pheasant, gutting them of entrails, dressing them, the odd inversion of this verb.

She walked beside federal buildings surrounded by lawns and then finally stores again and movie theaters and restaurants. She wandered this lively village, Westwood Village, its sidewalks teeming with people, students, she supposed, seeing their backpacks, their intense concentration on their wired devices, no doubt a university nearby. She noted their clothing, the girls, the tight black leggings, the short boots with their buckles clicking, a hermetic nonchalance, which would never be her, she realized, she a small clever opportunistic animal, too avid for nonchalance, a red fox making her way around the outskirts of the fairgrounds, and she laughed a little at herself, but she knew she needed to learn something about these instruments, something of these intensely focused fascinations that left people's faces so affectless, and she would learn, she would, she told herself, and then she drew close to the windows of a shop draped with pale green fabric, one curtain edge drawn aside just a foot or two to show a small round table upon which sat a three-tiered wedding cake. White clematis cascaded down the cake and vined around its base. They were made of sugar or paste or something, and they were careful and still and beautiful. A card held by a silver angel read *Georg* and beneath the name the words *gateaux d'occasion*, and beneath that a telephone number, and beneath that *by appointment*. She knew these flowers were clematis because her grandmother had planted a vine in the yard in Needles. The clematis had caused tension. Was it God's creation, an example of His beauty? Or was it idolatrous, yet something else to distract one's attention away from God? It would probably die now that she wasn't there to water it, to keep its feet moist, as her grandmother instructed, *They like moist feet and a sunny face.* Someday, a garden, she said to herself, and she thought of Julien Stoke's house in Santa Monica, the small yard in front, the loquat tree with its glowing yellow orbs. She began to scold herself, other people's possesssions, their lives. They weren't hers, couldn't be hers, and then she realized a driveway alongside the shop and a woman

—

unloading stacks of flat lucite boxes from her car parked with its hazard lights blinking, tray upon tray being handed off to a man in a white tee shirt standing at a side door. She walked up the driveway so that she could see more closely what was in the boxes. The woman and the man stopped and turned and looked at her, both holding stacked trays in their arms. She was a girl and they weren't afraid.

"I just wanted to see the flowers," she said. "They're really amazing. You made them?" she asked the woman, but the woman didn't answer, nor did the man. She smelled the bakery, the toast and the melting sugar smell within the flues, and she heard through the side door a buzzer going off and radio voices. "I can bake," she said, "or clean, or whatever you might need. May I have a job?" she asked, fatigue showing finally in her voice, fear perhaps.

"Who says 'May I have a job?'" the man asked, his voice heavily accented. He turned and disappeared and then returned to take the stack of clear boxes from the woman's hands. The woman pushed a section of her car key and the trunk clicked open and the woman retrieved more lucite trays and handed them off. Neither the woman nor the man spoke to her, and she stood awkwardly, waiting, but also curious at what she saw in the boxes, the various shades of purple and violet flowers, the leaves and the long lengths of stem. What were they made of?

Finally the woman turned, holding a stack of empty trays that the man had just handed to her, and asked on her way to her car's trunk, "What are you doing out this late at night? I'll give you a ride home. Just let me finish getting these."

The woman was small, smaller than she was, perhaps made even smaller-looking by the large white shirt with its cropped sleeves, and then she reached out to help the woman with the empties, stacking them carefully in the woman's trunk, and when this was full, continuing to place trays in the backseat of the woman's car. "Thank you," the woman said, looking somewhat keenly at her. "Put your knapsack in, sit. I'll be right back," the woman instructed her, and so she sat in the passenger seat, tentatively, with the car door hanging open, and she listened to the raised voices amid the radio voices, the woman's voice and the man's, angry, exasperated, both of them in contrast to the practiced bright airiness of the radio commentators and to the clicking of the hazard lights coming from the dashboard of the car.

Exhaustion encased her and she closed her eyes, smelled the sugar of the flowers, smelled rubber and plastic and carpet, and the ambient exhaust from the street; she smelled her own subtle particularity and the faint memory of the Florida Water in the bridge of her nose and within her forehead. She told herself she couldn't sleep, not yet. She reached out for the car door, pulled it snug against her shoulder, a prop, and then she rolled the window down, wanting the cold air to keep her awake, her will both fragile and great, but she fell anyway, collapsing heavily, immured within exhaustion. Her jaw set and her teeth ground themselves within the set of her jaw, and when she flinched awake, a thick forearm stretched before her eyes, its dark hair dusted with flour. She pushed back in the car seat and then could see the arm's hand holding one-hundred-dollar bills. The

—

woman sat beside her now, behind the wheel of her car, and the bills lingered in the air, the man's thick arm an inch from her nose.

"Don't frighten her," the woman said. "Stop that," and the man folded down and looked in the open car window at her, his face gigantic, pleasant, his eyes amused. Hundred-dollar bills floated for an instant in the dim light and then settled as she and the woman watched his broad white tee-shirted back retreat across the driveway and then pass through the side door of the bakery. The door closed and a cone of gray light superimposed itself, and then shut off, and now the entire length of the side wall of the building sat dark.

PROMOTION

I was a Walker, a volunteer for the Festival because I loved books, and it pleased my mother when I got out of the house and did something that "farthered my education." My job was to escort a Writer across the campus from the Green Room to his or her venue, to their reading or their book signing, or to just a Panel, if they weren't famous enough to have the other two. It was pleasant work, depending on the Writer, of course, and I now had a few signed books. I liked reading a book the author had signed, as though their hand were there with a pen for all time, its tip writing you into the book, pointing *here, here, begin here, I've written your name.* I never told my mother the word she wanted was "furthered" because that's when education and my mother's pride—or perhaps our culture—collided. No one as young as I am corrected her elders. Then again, I was happy to farther my education, too, as it was time to get out of the house. I loved my mother, but I was almost thirty-one and I wanted my own place, a studio apartment that I could line with books, so that everywhere I turned there was a book that I had either read or was about to read and it would be like living outside of time, outside of thirty-one-year-old Latina with a college degree still living at home with her mother.

"Hard Choices" was in the last-Panel-of-the-day slot and I was surprised at how many people were coming into the auditorium, walking down the aisles, picking rows, taking their seats. A bright silvered projection—LOS ANGELES FESTIVAL OF BOOKS—glowed hugely across the entire front of the stage just behind where the Writers, the Panelists, sat. This had been my third Walk of the day, and my last, and now I was seated to the side in the front row. I held my Writer's purse and sweater and a stack of books she'd brought with her, books written by the other Panelists. I could smell her perfume from her sweater, though I guess now that I was looking at the sweater, trying to fold it to keep it uncreased, it was more of a shawl. She seemed put together without seeming overly concerned about it, and that seemed precisely the look she was after, too. *You think I care? Fuck you, of course I care.* There was a sense of humor there, too, but for some reason I had a bad feeling about the next hour.

I can't say I thought the Festival had been going particularly well, but still I loved it. This year it was at a new venue, a different campus, and there seemed to be issues over the availability of books. One of my Walks poked in angry calls to his agent on his cell phone as we strode to Bovard Hall. This Author was a muckety-muck. "*Siren,*" he kept saying, "that's the only title they have." I tried to ask him how many titles the Festival was supposed to have had stocked, but he was on to the next call, focused, like one of his detectives. If I was splayed on the sidewalk, bloody, then he'd be interested. But I felt sorry for him, too. This was his livelihood, a business that supported his family, and he was here to sell a brand, not just one book title. I got that, not that that was difficult to get.

—

All of the afternoon Panelists were women, women of a certain age, like somehow that had been part of the "hard choice," to be women writers of a certain age. I didn't know, but gossip in the Green Room had it that "Hard Choices" had been scheduled for tomorrow, Sunday, the last day of the Festival and in the last Panel slot. Someone had complained and now it was today and people were coming in. It was hard to know why they were here or what this Panel was about, or what the audience was expecting. I didn't know, and certainly no one was asking my opinion. I was just a Walker.

"When I introduce you, you hold up your book," the Moderator said into the microphone, tilting her head and gazing down the long narrow table at the three Panelists. In the Moderator's inflection, her instruction, it was just understood how sensible and straightforward an idea this was. The Panelist sitting closest to her nodded her head, as did another Panelist sitting beside her. My Panelist way down at the far end of the table didn't respond. Anyone watching—and I was watching—could see she'd hold up her book in this Show-and-Tell fashion when Chernobyl became inhabitable again. That was about twenty-two thousand years from now.

My Panelist sat farthest from the Moderator and the other Panelists because to sit more to the middle of the long narrow table on the stage was to have a very bright light shining in her eyes, the light that projected LOS ANGELES FESTIVAL OF BOOKS across the front of the small auditorium. The light had blinded her, and blue-eyed, her eyes spasmed and closed against the glare. She had gotten up and moved her chair as far out of the light as possible. This seemed sensible enough to me, but I could see that the Moderator was fussed; she didn't want my Panelist on the other end of the stage.

"This needs to be turned off," the Moderator said, looking to the Volunteers in their yellow tee shirts, and then to the Tech Guy in the corner running the computers, the "smart" techonology. He shrugged his white tee-shirted shoulders and changed which buttock he was perched on. "This is not negotiable," the Moderator said, trying to be forceful, and one of the Volunteers in her yellow tee shirt, a round-faced woman with dark hair and heavily slowed movements said, "This is the first anyone has complained about it all day."

I watched my Panelist roll her eyes, and though I was sure most people would think her a class-A bitch, I didn't read her roll that way. I thought she was saying to herself, *Figures that I'd be the only one who didn't want to sit in the intense glare of a projector bulb—figures.* I could see that she was used to being some kind of oddity. She sat down there at the far end without looking uncomfortable or out of place or awkward. Maybe she was even used to being alone. On that score, I was unsure. Coming from the Green Room across campus to this small auditorium, she'd been nice to me, taking off her sunglasses and looking at me when she asked me questions. Did I go to school here? Was I a graduate student? Did I like to read? Did I myself write? I told her that I kept the books for my uncle's pretty successful chain of Oaxacan restaurants; I told her this was like having my brain seized and held hostage by an algorithm. She smiled at that. I had wanted to ask her about the dog in her book, had he really died that way? but I got shy and tongue-tied and didn't want her thinking I'd cared only for him. Somehow that seemed like something only a fool would ask. There was plenty of other stuff in this book, but that dog—I just couldn't shake this dog, what had happened to him, what he'd done.

The small auditorium was quieting down and the Volunteer in the yellow tee shirt was suggesting that the Panel get under way. The audience in the front rows had been listening to these exchanges about the projector light and many of them kept turning around and looking at the glare and then looking forward, waiting to see what would be done. The middle Panelist decided in her good-natured way that she didn't much like fighting the light either and so she got up and moved down the three yards to sit next to my Panelist at the far end. Now, five long white yards of table stretched between the one Panelist near the Moderator and the other two Panelists. It looked like a table at a banquet which no one had much bothered themselves to attend, and those who had bothered might actually have been the Waiters hired for the affair, sitting down, just hanging until Management sent them home.

The Moderator did begin, naming the Panelists and saying a few things she'd gotten off the Internet. Snippets from reviews. The Moderator was a Blogger. My Panelist didn't hold up her book. The Panelists were each invited to read an opening paragraph from one of their novels, and they all read pretty well, all seasoned pros, you could hear it in their pacing, slow, as if they actually knew what the words meant. It was lovely to be read to. I think the middle Panelist, the one who seemed so pleasant—so good-natured—she was rumored to be the one who'd complained about the time slot.

The Moderator asked a few questions and after a while it was obvious the Moderator hadn't actually read the books. The Moderator asked my Panelist why she wrote in second person and my Panelist leaned into her microphone and said curtly, "I don't." Then my Panelist did try to help the Moderator out a bit, suggesting that she wrote a point-of-view that people often mistook for first person, though it was actually third person. I knew the Moderator had second person, or "you," in her mind because all she'd read were online interviews. When the Moderator asked my Panelist about her screenplays, it was over.

"I don't write screenplays," my Panelist said, and then she looked at her watch and I could see sadness hanging across her eyes like drapes. I was exasperated, too, because one of the other Panelists wrote about the Donner Party, about Tamsen Donner, and how the hell the Moderator could not see that as a source of terrific interest was a little astounding. I hadn't finished that book, but I think the Donner Party—before they'd had to start snacking on one another—had made the decision, a "hard choice," if you will, to take a short cut through the Sierra Nevadas. It seemed odd that this wasn't being talked about. It was certainly something that would interest people in buying the book.

Unfortunately the question presently afoot was whether or not characters' names were important? I didn't think the Panelist who wrote on the Donner Party had named many

of her characters; I think she'd pretty much stuck close to
the historical record, but—being fairly patient and kind—
she allowed that character names were important. I resolved
that I'd ask my Panelist my questions on the way back to the
Green Room. Even what her perfume was called, just to get
things started. The scent was another side to her, I thought,
deep and earthy but floral, too. I bet there's a word for it, for
this combination of smells, but I didn't know it. I wanted to
know about the dog, and I wanted her to sign my book and I
was hoping she wouldn't be upset about this stupid panel, but
somehow I knew she wouldn't be; she was too sad for that.
I looked at her now and her eyes seemed recessed as though
looking back into herself for some lost ability, some resource
of graciousness she'd once had. She rotated her wrist again,
eyeing her watch. I knew my mother would like her; the
Moderator hated her guts.

Finally there were some intelligent questions from the
audience, or rather what was left of the audience. People had
gotten up and left during the panel and I wasn't surprised; it
was all pretty silly until the Q & A. Then time was called and
it was over, and people were filing out and gone and the Panelists were off the stage to the side speaking to one another in a
huddle, and then signing the books my Panelist had come and
gotten from me. She had two books by each of the other Writers, nice hardbacks, and each of the Writers had a knee arched
up and was leaned over, signing their books to her. My Panelist gestured to me, *Was she keeping me from something?* and I
shook my head no. I was happy waiting; I had my questions.

—

At the front of the auditorium LOS ANGELES FESTIVAL OF BOOKS glowed hugely, sending out over the empty seats its oblivious beatific light.

The Panelists—the Writers—were theoretically all supposed to be escorted to a little tent area where they would sit each in their own tent and sign books. But there hadn't been books to buy anywhere that I could see and my Panelist coming across the floor looked at me and smiled quietly. *Let's go*, her eyes said, and I took back the stack of books from her without asking and she reached for her purse and shawl. "I don't see any point in dragging this out, do you?" she asked me.

I didn't want to agree with her because it might seem like a reflection on her book, or like I was saying yeah, this was all a bust, but the book-signing tents were in this rather faraway location, and I didn't think anyone *would* be there now, not for her nor for the other Writers, either. The Panel had been dismal, and other than refusing to hold up her book, I thought my Panelist had done what she was supposed to do to promote her book—she'd been here, ready, and when a woman in the audience had asked about her research on an earlier book, she'd been expansive, even generous. But this made me a little angry, too, because it showed she could have turned this entire thing around, that she could have livened up the stage. My Panelist obviously knew enough about the other books to have broached some better questions, and I wondered that she hadn't pulled out of herself enough to show the Moderator what a good question was. Even if she couldn't do it for herself, she could have done it for the other writers, helped showcase them more. But my Panelist was weary too, and, it seemed, weary of people being angry at her, and it really wasn't her responsibility to ask the questions, or to moderate.

"We can just go back to the Green Room, can't we?" my Panelist asked now. "I won't get you in trouble, right?" I shook my head and she turned and walked quickly up the aisle. "Thank you for folding my shawl," she said over her shoulder.

"I'm surprised you're not a little mad," I said to her, following her brisk footsteps, catching up to her. "Most writers would be angry."

"Oh," she said, and then laughed a little and winked at me. "Why, are most writers real divas?"

I thought about this question, wanted to tell her some of the behavior I'd seen, but it didn't seem decorous of me, and anyway, she wasn't asking for gossip, and then the time of the question's pressing was over.

We walked down the steps of the building and into the courtyard strewn with the purple blossoms of jacarandas. "They are particularly beautiful this year, aren't they? The rain," she added. "We've had so much rain."

I thought of Holy Week in Ajijic, where my mother is from, of the cobblestone streets strewn with alfalfa and jacaranda, and the old village women making their way to the cathedral on their bloodied knees and their knees becoming more and more encrusted with the green grass and the crushed purple blossoms. I remembered seeing this for the first time as a child and being horrified and fascinated.

"Hock-a-rahnda," my Writer said, pronouncing it correctly

—

in Spanish, rolling saliva into it at the back of her throat. "It drove my father crazy that we always mispronounced it. He spoke perfect Spanish."

"Yeah, well I don't," I said.

I was about to ask her about her perfume when she thrust up her arms, saying "What way?!" in mock exasperation. She was making a joke because we were walking down Watt Way, and all day long, because the maps for the Festival had been so hard to decipher, people had been saying, *What way? Where do we go? How do you get there?* and so What Way or Watt Way was funny.

"Oaxacan," she said, "that's moles, right? Where they originate from?" but she didn't wait for me to tell her differently. "I understand," she said without preamble. "Cultural stereotype. Good or bad, it doesn't much matter, and yet they operate sometimes."

I didn't know what she was referring to, but I supposed "Mexican" had to be part of it. I didn't say anything because A, it wasn't my place to say much, and B, she wasn't about to say anything mean, I could tell.

"At Forest Lawn Cemetery, after my husband died, the person assigned to help me with the arrangements reminds me of you."

"Oh," I said, because I didn't really know what was coming? Day of the Dead shit or how Mexicans accept death better than other cultures. It wasn't going to be mean, but it probably wasn't going to be some mind-blowing perception, either. We had started down Childs Way toward the famous bronze statue of Tommy Trojan, the school's mascot.

—

"Just that," she said firmly, pushing up her sunglasses. "She was about your age, and she was very kind to me . . . and then she was replaced because the director said we'd never get it all managed at the rate we were going. She was almost as distraught as I was."

Yeah, yeah, I thought, big plump Latina girls—all heart, whatever, that's why they end up taking care of everyone's children along with their own, but my Writer didn't say anymore. Finally, I had to ask, "So, what happened?'

"Nothing," she said, "nothing that hadn't already happened."

We were started down the narrow wooded path that led past the chapel and then onto Town & Gown where the Green Room was. "I mean, what happened with the arrangements, the person who was supposed to help you?"

"They gave me a tough little Korean woman," she said, stepping off the path, which was strewn with jacaranda blossoms, too. "We got it all done," she added, "but what was the hurry?"

We both exchanged looks, stymied, like truth was a cul-de-sac sometimes, or a vortex; there was only one way it was all going to go.

"I love this little chapel," she then said, pointing. "Can we go in for a moment?"

I told her yes, of course we could, and when we got to the old wooden door, I opened it for her and we both scraped from our shoes as well as we could the crushed purple blossoms. We sat down on the front pew in the dim cool light and I set the stack of books written by the other Panelists between us.

"Want me to sign that," she asked, nodding at the copy of

her book I'd had in the pocket of my jacket all day. "If you don't want me to, that's okay," she went on. "I think some people don't like their books sullied." She settled her purse and shawl in a puddle on the pew and then quietly, looking up at the stained-glass window, she said, "—and you want to know something, maybe something about my dog?"

She hadn't really spoken about her writing before in those terms, like "my dog," or "my life," and I knew she'd let her guard down, that she wasn't being an author right now, but just a person. I had this thought that we were like two people sitting on a bench in a park talking and the book was this monument or statue nearby, some historical thing I knew a lot about, and it didn't really matter that she had been the person to make it. It was over there and she was here, on the bench, her hands in her lap.

"What does your name mean?" she asked, looking closely at my name tag. "Strong? Or maybe it actually means a fort?"

"Or a battle horse," I said, "if you can believe that?" I didn't take her book from my jacket pocket and hand it to her.

"Sure, I can believe that," and we both laughed because somehow "Latina" was back in play. She then stood up and looked down at me. "I need to let you go, don't I? It's Saturday—almost Saturday evening! But yes, all true. He was a dog of a higher order, you could say."

"I don't have a date or anything," I said. "You don't have to worry." She looked at me squint-eyed and I gave in. "Not till later."

"Whew," she said, dragging her hand across her forehead. "Don't make it hard for us old folks to live vicariously."

She could be pretty funny and it occurred to me that the Moderator had gotten off easy because I knew this woman could also hand people their heads on platters. "You're not old," I said. "Come on—don't make it easy for young people to be crass."

She smiled delightedly at this, her face open, and I could see in for just a second, a bright sunroom at the back of the house.

"So, what do you really want to do with your life," she asked, bending down and pulling her book from my jacket pocket. I wasn't sure I liked her doing this. I mean, it was her book and everything . . . but it was my book . . . and everything, too. "I'm not sure I espy the soul of an accountant," she added, by way of goading, and then she apologized immediately. "You don't have to answer," she said, handing me back my book. "You're the one person who bought a book, and you bought it, what? two weeks ago?"

"Sign my book," I said. "Please. I want you to."

". . . and it is your book now, isn't it," she said, talking herself into something, perhaps some distance she wasn't sure she'd ever be able to have. "I'm right, though, yes?" she asked, taking the book back from me. She leaned down and rummaged in her purse. She then held a long green pencil case, or pen case, and she unzipped it and lifted out a beautiful black fountain pen. She walked off a few paces into the quiet mood of the chapel. I watched her hunch a little, the book propped in her left hand. She was signing the book on its last page, writing something, cocking her head, reading it over.

I stood up as she was coming back and then I reached out to

—

her and hugged her closely. She smelled so good, but she didn't feel quite alive, and then I didn't know whether I was hugging her because I loved her book or because I wanted her to be happier, or because I was a big sweet Latina, too. It was all a jumble. But not the book. Now, somehow, I knew that everything I'd felt about the book was true. Not true to her, but true to the book, and she handed it to me as we came apart, my book.

SHE

She gathered the one-hundred-dollar bills in the dark car without being asked to do so, and then she counted them, and then counted them again, their metalic smell in the air. "Eight," she said. "I count eight." The woman didn't say anything for a time, just sat looking through the windshield, her hands resting on the steering wheel, and then she could see the woman's hands shaking, shaking but grasping harder in order to stop the shaking. Finally, the woman turned to her and looked across the short distance of the car, and then she knew to say to the woman something, almost anything, and so she said, "You made those white clematis in the window, didn't you?"

"Yes," the woman said simply. "I made them, but those," she gestured behind her vaguely where the front window of the bakery might be, "those I made as a demo, let's call it, a little sampling so that Georg could show the world what he can do. He's never paid me for those. Those are free and clear of monetary exchange! Want to go for a drive?" the woman asked, turning the key in the car's ignition. "I have a delivery to make downtown." The woman then let out a huge sigh. "Oh God, what am I saying? Where do you live?"

"I don't," she said quietly. "Where would you like me to put these?"

The woman reached across and drew the bills from her hands as though she hadn't heard what she'd said, and then the woman leaned down unnervingly close to her bare knees in the passenger-side footwell and opened the glove compartment. The woman lifted out a woven pouch and zippered it open and folded the bills inside and then returned it into the dark alcove. The woman hesitated, the glove compartment door hanging open, and then she turned the car ignition off and pulled out the key and closed the glove compartment and locked it.

"I need to deliver some shit," the woman said, her small hands now quieted and her shoulders slumped down against the steering wheel, her voice muffled. "Actually, it's ganache, ganache in various shades of shit. You wanted a job!"

She looked at the woman's narrow back, her shoulder blades lifting the thin fabric of her white shirt. She could see the woman was tired. They both were. "What is ganache?" she asked. What she really wanted to say was that she would not steal the woman's money.

"I shouldn't really call it that because I stabilize it with gelatin. It's really more of an Italian cream."

"Okay," she said. "I know what gelatin is."

"That's a start," the woman said, laughing now, raising herself from the steering wheel and sitting back in her seat. "It's a kind of crazy show, a little . . . well, I don't know . . . there's masked wrestling and musicians, very traditional Mexican ranchera, and Mayan dancers, strippers even, and this very beautiful male stripper, well you don't know he's a man until the end—but in one act a wrestler smears shit all over the referees."

"They do?" she asked. The idea seemed so alien, so far out

—

of her reach, that she couldn't quite rein it into sense, into the woman's seeming ease with it.

"It's chocolate," the woman said hurriedly. "Ganache. It's not really shit, but the wrestler carries a baggie of it in his tights and at the right moment he digs into his behind and acts as though he's defecated in his hand and then slings it at the referee."

She didn't know what to say. Of all the many times she'd been angry, this as a recourse had never occurred to her, and she thought that maybe this was a good thing, something perhaps right about her, a sign of maturity, but she didn't really know even what to think about such an act, or that this woman made it possible, that this woman made beautiful white clematis and what she guessed would be called chocolate feces.

"It's actually pretty funny," the woman ventured, looking sideways at her. "It's real carnival, and they've had so much fun slinging the shit, they need more. I have to drive it downtown, okay?"

"Would you tell me what's in it?" she asked. "How you make it?"

"Egg yolks, cream, chocolate, gelatin."

"That's it?"

"That's it," the woman said, fitting the key back in the ignition. "Though I think we're going to change it up a bit, put some flour in for weight, so it flies farther. It won't be quite as tasty for the referee if they make him eat it that night, but it will fling with more direction."

"Okay," she said, looking down at her hands in the dim

—

light, her hands that would never open this glove compartment and take the woman's money, *not enough money anyway*, she thought to herself, not what she wanted, not even what she needed. What would eight hundred dollars buy her? A few nights in a motel? And even that she supposed she'd need identification for. She began to be able to see her white tennis shoes in the darkness of the footwell, a lot more scuffed now, a lot more trodded within, but still invitations to geography, to movement, to seeking her life. She was attempting to buoy herself, to remind herself of the promise of these white tennis shoes. She had kept them pristine for weeks, and especially for this trip, for this bolting. If she had to bolt farther, she would, her white shoes carrying her. And there was always the tremendous propulsion of her anger, its ability to sustain her, to sanction her.

She had had her day of luxuriant anonymity, this remarkable float . . . and now she supposed she needed a name. "Okay," she said again, aloud, to the woman. *A name*, she said to herself, though the idea of this word or words seemed extraneous to her, a drag upon her momentum. But perhaps a name now would help her? That she had even thought to take the woman's money alarmed her. That she had calculated the money's reach, imagined a future in which she had bought herself a place to sleep for a night, two nights, maybe three with someone else's money, and she a thief . . . She could not be anonymous, let alone luxuriantly so, and a thief. Perhaps a name would help her leave this mistake behind, even if this mistake had just been a momentary thought.

"I can see you're a bit stunned," the woman said. "It's harmless, or better said, it's a great outlet for a lot of anger and anxiety and frustration."

"Is that true? I've never thought to do that to anyone."

"Monkeys do it all of the time."

"Still, I've just never—"

"I'm kidding you."

"How do you know that?"

"About the monkeys? You haven't ever been to a zoo? The monkey section—the shit's flying."

She heard the easy equation between monkeys and humans, between their behavior and that of humans, and so as far away as she was from anything she knew about, she was also back in it, her father's anger at scientists, evolution, his insistence on God as the source of all things. Sometimes, when he wasn't angry, she understood his desire to have one answer to all things, she did, but his answer was at the expense of so much, and so harmful to so many. Once she'd said to him that she understood he was afraid to die, afraid to cease being, the horror of imagining nonexistence. She said she understood why heaven was so consoling to him. He had reached for her hands and pulled the pad of each of her fingertips down the edge of the gas bill, slicing methodically all ten pads with paper cuts, daring her to ever patronize him again. *Patronize.* She had asked her grandmother what that meant, and her grandmother had laughed, saying, "That's his own hell, darling girl, what he wants and doesn't want at the same time. Plenty of lovely men, but your father isn't one of

them. Promise me that you don't forget that there are lovely
men in the world."

"What do you mean you don't live anywhere," the woman
asked her now, backing her car down the drive. "You're not a
street person, I can see that."

"I took my leave this morning of everything I have ever
known." The words sounded stiff and formal, and she liked
their sound, the formality like a wall that she now stood safely
behind. "Past life," she said, "and now I need very much a place
to stay tonight . . ."

"And a job."

"Tomorrow, yes, a job—"

"But tonight a bed . . ."

"Yes, tonight a bed."

"You can't just toss up in a city and expect people to take
you in." The woman's voice sounded exasperated, frantic. The
woman looked straight ahead, out the windshield of her car,
watching for the light to turn, waiting to accelerate, her jaw
firm to her chore, or to her fathoming. "I think it's illegal, for
one thing."

"Illegal to help someone?"

"Almost, yes."

"Harboring a minor."

"Well, put that way, I like the sound of it," the woman said,
and then they both laughed together quietly, some immediate
connection, the language, the word "harboring," harbor, its
seeming endurance.

"It is my birthday tomorrow."

"Is that true?"

She didn't answer because the next question would be, what number? or, how old would she be? "It could be a floor," she said, "or a couch. Would you do that for me?" she asked, and then she said for reasons she would never know, "I had a grandmother," and the woman said quietly in the dim car, "I had a mother."

The streets streaked past. They drove for a time within a corridor of lumbering high-rise apartment buildings and then beside huge department stores with brilliant windows full of dummy women with long prosthetic-looking legs, one forward, one leaned upon, the clothes exotic, silly, and then the language changed and the woman told her it was Korean. The woman pointed out what she called her favorite misspelling, an automotive shop selling "muffrers." The woman supposed it was a bit racist to be amused, the phonetic spelling of a Korean pronunciation, but maybe it was harmless, too? Then the language of the signs changed again, to Spanish now, and then Greek, and then Spanish again, and they turned a corner and parked cars hopped up and down with music blaring joyously from their open windows. "Banda," the woman said, "and maybe you'll get to hear some rancheras, mariachi. Or maybe you just want to wait?" she asked. "I'll just be a minute." The woman turned the car into a lot across the street. Parking attendants in black vests swarmed, yelling, cheering, *"Hola, Choco-caca! Hola!"* and the woman turned to her and said, "You have to come and see. I know you're tired."

She smiled, watching the long chrome-bright American

—

233

cars bounce and dive and lunge and spring back, their windows all down, the music raucous. The woman said, "Hydraulics. Don't ask me exactly, but they've installed hydraulic pumps in the suspension of their cars—I think?—but I'm no mechanic."

"You'll teach me, yes, to make the flowers you make? I'm good with my hands—I made five dollars today hemming a woman's dress, and she'll pay me more because I helped her tonight, at an opening, an art opening, but you'll teach me."

The woman had pulled her car behind other cars where she was directed to by the attendants, all waving her in grandly. She leaned forward and turned off the engine. "Stay in the car," she said. "You'll be fine. These guys are sweet, and you'll see this another time. I'll be right back," and she reached the keys to the glove compartment and unlocked it and brought out the woven pouch that held her money.

"I wouldn't ever steal from you. Here," she said to the woman, and she leaned down and pulled the five dollars from her backpack. The bill seemed suspended in the dim light of the car. "I can stay with you? Tonight? Even just one night? I'm no thief."

The woman lightly pushed her hand away. "Maybe you're not exactly sure what you are?" The woman was now twisting around, struggling to pull a soft cooler case from behind her seat. "That's okay," the woman said into her own shoulder, twisting her body around even more acutely. "I was once a botanist—maybe I still am—and now I make sugar flowers, and somehow through no doing of my own, I now have a partner."

—

234

"I don't know jack," she said to the woman, who was now on her knees, leaned over into the backseat, unzipping the case.

"Right," the woman said, distracted, pulling one white tub from the cooler and then another and turning back around and settling them between her knees, one atop the other. "What's that? Short for Jacqueline—I'll be right back," she said, placing the woven pouch and her car keys atop the white tubs.

"*Choco-caca!*" the parking attendants yelled as the woman pushed her car door open. The music blared happily from the spastic cars across the street and there was laughter and the gnashing of the car door closing, and in her own breath an abrupt hitch because the guys were drumming on the roof of the car, teasing her inside it, "Hey, the baby sister! where you been?" and they leaned in toward the windows and waved at her and walked off, patting the pockets of their vests, and her heart settled and she could breathe in the small adequate space.

ACKNOWLEDGMENTS

So joyously many to thank, who sustain me, contain me, care for me. Not always an easy chore for them. Elizabeth Tallent, Joy Harris, Erika Goldman, who keep changing my life; Rhoda Huffey, whose tremendous affection keeps me here; Susan Segal, Jayne Lewis, Bruce McKay, Varley O'Connor, Molly Bendall, Andrew Tonkovich, Lisa Alvarez, Claudia Nadine—all my readers, all my friends, thank you, and my love and gratitude to many colleagues who are also friends, Linda Georgianna, Bob Newsom, Laura O'Connor, and Ron Carlson who shakes his big beautiful head at me with such a mixture of sadness and surprise; Hugh Roberts and Rachel Gamby, my dearest friends, and Vicki, whose words are always pure gold to me though her last name is Silver. Thank you to Michael Ryan whose words from the back of the room after I had read "Spa" aloud will always be with me; words from poets—I hoard those. Elizabeth Allen, thank you for making me feel stronger about "Out," which is a birthday present for Marisa Matarazzo, who deserves better presents, alas. Matt Sumell, for his pure heart, his friendship, his care, and Amanda Foushee, Joe Boone and Bill Handley, the keenest minds, the warmest friends, and you all keep me laughing, no easy feat that. Thank you to Vicki Forman, who is there, always there, and to Brett Hall Jones, and Arielle Read Giordano, who recently knitted me the most beautiful shawl. It represents her arms around me—I will never forget how you took care of me,

—

237

and continue to. Many a Sunday I see my friend Kim Ennis at the farmers' market, and as she bags people's Lolla Rossa and pipicha, and hands them back their change, we talk around their shoulders and over their heads about books. So fun! Thank you.

I have two families, Paul's and my own, and these families extend, there's bj and Mardi, too. Just know how much you all mean to me. How much I depend upon you. Thank you for continuing to claim me.

I want to thank en masse the writers in the Programs In Writing at UC Irvine, who give me a place to be every week, who trust me—for the most part—with their fine work, and whose brightness lights my days. And thank you to Laura Swendson who many a day in the last two years has said to me, "you're supposed to be writing—I'll do this." Bless you.

John Glusman. "It's called a disc player, Michelle." I don't know why that has made me laugh so much, but it has. Thank you for the teasing. Thank you for your wise and incredibly respectful editing. I'm still trying to come up with answers to some of your brilliant questions; I wish I were brilliant enough to answer them. Thank you for my new home, and to Alexa Pugh, and to all at W. W. Norton & Company for putting this book in the world with such care.